A VERY HERO WEDDING

The Justice Thalia Stories
Snowfall
Murder Most Fowl
The Sweetest Poison
A Granddaughter of Mine

Tales of the Twelve
The Trickster Priestess and the Demon

888-555-HERO
Hero De Facto
Hero Ad Hoc
Hero De Novo
A Very Hero Christmas
Hero De Jure
Hero In Camera
Hero Amicus Curiae
A Very Hero Wedding
A Very Hero New Year
Hero Ad Litem
Queer Eye for the Super Guy

Solar System Services, Inc.
Alone Is Not Lonely

Millersburg Magick Mysteries
Spells and Sleuths
Fae and Felonies
Magick and Murder

Soccer Moms of the Apocalypse
Pestilence in Pumpkin Spice
Famine In French Vanilla
War in White Chocolate
Death in Double Mocha

Miscellaneous
Sword and Sorceress 31 ("Pig-Headed")
Sword and Sorceress 32 ("Unexpected")
Practical Witches
Revenge Served Hot
The Yule Switch
Chocolate for Dinner
Silver Shoes and Pigs' Ears

For updates, news, and giveaways, join Suzan's mailing list or visit her website at www.suzanharden.com. You can also check her out on Twitter or Facebook.

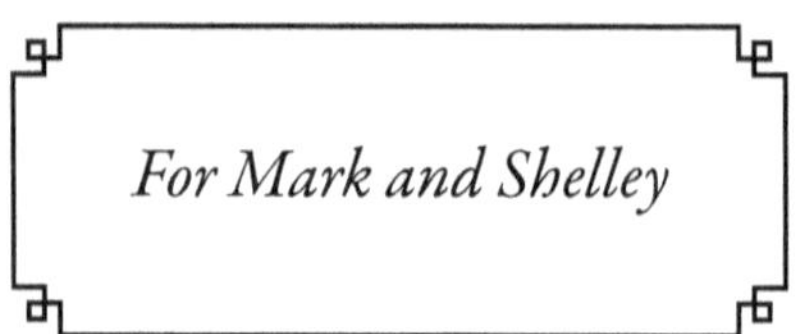

This is a work of fiction. All characters, organizations and events in this novel are products of the author's imagination and are not to be construed as real. Any resemblance to persons, living or dead, is entirely coincidental.

A VERY HERO WEDDING (888-555-HERO #8)
Copyright 2021 by Suzan Harden
All rights reserved
ISBN-13 - 978-1-938745-97-3

Published by Angry Sheep Publishing
Findlay, Ohio

Interior Design by JW Manus
Cover Design by For the Muse Designs

A Very Hero Wedding

888-555-HERO #8

Suzan Harden

Chapter 1

<hr>

The heat inside the Lechuza Building didn't match the last blaze of sweltering summer in Canyon Pointe. No, the heat inside was much worse despite the chilled air pumping from the building's ancient ventilation system. Nor could it be soothed by the iced version of Aisha Franklin's favorite no-fat, sugar-free peppermint mocha.

As much as she wanted to see her blood kin at her baby brother's wedding, she wished she could leave her adopted family behind. She glared at her law partner and best friend, Harri Winters, who sat across their office conference room table.

"We need someone to cover the office. We can't leave for a week with no one—" Aisha began.

Again.

"Then find someone we can trust!" Harri yelled.

"I said I would stay—" Susan Kennedy, their third and newest partner, started to say.

"No!" Aisha and Harri shouted at the same time.

Loud banging filled the room before Patty Ames, their legal assistant and all-around Girl Friday, shoved the door open. Blue eyes blazed from beneath her wayward blond curls. "Keep it down in here. The clients on the phone can hear you."

Patty didn't yell. She used what their building manager's four sons referred to as her "Mommy-growly" voice. Not even Aisha's husband Rey or her brother-in-law Steve messed with Patty when she used that voice, and they were both supers.

"We're sorry," Aisha said. "We'll be quieter."

"Harri?" Patty's voice carried an obvious warning. Ever since her daughter Grace was born, their assistant acted more and more like the firm's boss.

Or the partners' mother.

"I'll be quiet, Patty," Harri grumbled.

"Thank you." Patty closed the conference room door behind her.

"All I'm saying is opposing counsel will use the opportunity of the office being closed to pull shenanigans," Aisha said.

"Because that's what you'd do," Harri snapped.

"Isn't that the pot calling the kettle black?" Susan asked. When Aisha glared at her, Susan held up her palms. "Was that racist? I swear I wasn't going there."

Aisha blew out a deep breath and decided to ignore the jibe. "Too bad Steve isn't licensed yet. We could stick him with desk duty as the newbie."

"Why don't we?" Susan said. "He's not going to Martin's wedding because of classes. He's taking the legal clinic at the law school next year. Let's give him the experience. If something happens and he needs a licensed attorney, he can call one of us."

Aisha exchanged looks with Harri. "It's a good idea. I'll fly home if there's a major problem."

"You can't," Harri said. "It's your brother's wedding."

"You can't," Aisha replied. "It's your foster brother's wedding."

Susan waved her arms. "Excuse me! I said I would stay from the beginning!"

"Shhhhh!" Aisha and Harri said at the same time.

Harri glanced over her shoulder, but the conference room door didn't open. She looked at Susan. "You don't want her back in here yelling at us, do you?"

"So, we're agreed?" Aisha said. "Steve handles the phones except when he's in class?"

"What about when he's not in class?" Harri asked.

"What about Javier's friend Josie?" Aisha suggested.

Harri shook her head. "She's finally back in school. I don't mind giving her odd jobs around the building on the weekends and summer, but I am not giving her an excuse to drop out. What about her mom Veronica? Javier said something about her losing her job again."

Aisha slowly nodded. "Yeah, that might work." Like a lot of people in the neighborhood, Veronica had grabbed her kids and fled north because of trouble in Central America. In their case, Veronica's family had immigrated legally. However, Veronica had a lot of trouble getting her teaching certification in the U.S. She fell into a downward spiral her pride and American prejudice wouldn't let her pull out of. Maybe this was a chance to do some good. "I'll talk to her."

"I can do it," Harri said.

"Your Spanish sucks," Aisha and Susan said in unison.

"She's going to need to speak English when answering the phone," Harri snapped.

"She's going react more positively to someone she thinks is one of her own," Aisha said. "Someone who speaks like a native. Do you realize you have a British accent when you speak Spanish?"

"I've been—" Harri started loudly. When Aisha hissed and pointed at the door, Harri lowered the volume of her voice. "I've been practicing."

"I'll talk with Veronica," Aisha insisted.

"You mean the Ghost Owl will talk with Veronica." Harri crossed her arms and sulked.

"The Ghost Owl will get through to her better than a bunch of stuck-up gringa lawyers," Susan said.

"She's got a point," Aisha said.

"Fine," Harri said while she stood. "Anything else we need to talk about?"

Both Aisha and Susan shook their heads.

"Fine," Harri repeated before she stomped out of the conference room.

"What the hell crawled up her butt?" Susan muttered. "It's just a wedding. I'm not even sure why your brother invited me."

"This isn't about the wedding," Aisha replied.

"You've got to be kidding me." Susan flopped against the back of her chair and rolled her eyes. "She's still pissed about you accompanying Rey to Paris?"

"Unfortunately." Aisha tapped her nails against the conference table. Harri better get her shit sorted before they flew to Atlanta on Friday for Martin's wedding.

Otherwise, Aisha might just drop her best friend from thirty thousand feet.

CHAPTER 2

Harri stomped back into her office and slammed the door. Why the hell didn't Aisha get the fact their fledgling law firm was too new for a partner to take a year off? Because no matter what she said about remote working from Paris while Rey attended culinary school, they couldn't take the chance of Mitch developing his powers around some French au pair.

Which meant Aisha would need to be a full-time mother. Plus, there was the time difference between the western United States and France. There was simply no way for her to continue practicing law full-time no matter what she said.

Harri threw herself in her office chair and stared at the pile of paperwork sitting in her to-do box. The firm had too much business as it was. They had been turning away potential clients over the summer after they successfully defended Ultramegaperson on charges of mass murder in the Golden Gate Bridge collapse last spring. While she'd spent most of her professional life in the city legal department, she was all too aware of what happened to any type of business that grew too fast.

She'd thrown every last cent she had into starting up this firm. Worse, she knew she couldn't do this without Aisha. Sure, Susan was a decent IP attorney, but Aisha's knowledge and expertise of superhero law outstripped both Harri and Susan put together. Not to mention the endorsements of Aisha's superhero persona and her job as a legal analyst at Channel 12 gave her additional income streams. Something Harri didn't have.

Was that the real problem? Was she jealous that Aisha earned more money than she did? But Aisha had always earned more since they graduated from law school because she'd gone into the private sector. If it didn't matter before, why did it matter now?

A slight knock on the office door intruded on Harri's pouting fit. She took a deep breath before she called out, "Come in!"

The aroma of fresh-brewed coffee and cinnamon entered before Patty with a steaming cup. She closed the office door before she strode over to Harri's desk and replaced the empty mug on the coaster with the fresh cup. Harri looked inside the cup before she eyed Patty.

Her assistant shrugged. "I've noticed you've been digging into the cinnamon syrup when you're having a bad day."

Damn. Harri resisted the urge to roll her eyes. She'd tried something new a few times, and now, Patty believed it's what she wanted all the time. Steve was smart enough to bring Harri her preferred straight black first thing in the morning, but he was back in classes since the new semester started last month. However, she couldn't take her pissy mood out on the younger woman. Patty was trying to support her, and Harri needed Patty's work skills even more than she needed Aisha's.

"Thank you," Harri said as she picked up the mug. "Did you need something in particular?"

"I thought you might want to talk." Patty sat in one of the visitor chairs, her fingers clenched around the empty cup. "That was a pretty bad argument among you guys this morning. Not a good sign when all three partners are yelling at each other like that."

"I know." Harri sighed and sipped her cinnamon coffee. It was definitely a flavor that could become an addiction, though right now, she'd prefer a shot of whiskey in her mug. "I'm really sorry about that."

Patty cocked her head. "Is this a serious problem, or is it your abandonment issues rearing their head again?"

Harri swallowed her defensive streak and considered the situation. Everyone in the building had called her on her emotional issues at one time or another, but only Patty had lost her parents at a young age like Harri had, and Patty was the most likely to listen, instead of judge.

"It's probably a little of both, but definitely serious if we lose a partner," Harri admitted.

Patty cocked her head. "So why are you doing your damnedest to chase Aisha away?"

Harri paused in mid-sip. "I'm not trying to chase her away. I'm pointing out why this Paris thing isn't a good idea."

"You also promised all of us you'd hire an associate this year, and it's the second week of September." Patty crossed her arms. "Instead, you've been trying to push me to go to law school. You've dumped a ton of work on Steve, who's not technically a second-year law student until the end of December. Not to mention, Aisha's been pulling more than her fair share of the load while being a new mother and a superhero."

Guilt poked at Harri's conscience. Was that the problem? Aisha did everything perfectly. Sweet kid. Gorgeous husband. Awesome triple career.

All while Harri could barely keep it together with one career and a boyfriend. It had been different when they were both freshly divorced, no kids, and no one else to lean on besides each other and Jeremy.

Then there was the reality of running the business.

"Our firm isn't at the point where a partner can take a year's sabbatical," Harri protested. "Our doors have only been open for a little over fourteen months."

"Fifteen going on sixteen." Patty shook her head. "Will you ever be at a point were one of us could take some time off without you panicking?"

"Probably not," Harri reluctantly admitted.

"And that's your personal insecurity talking." Patty leaned her elbows on Harri's desk. "What are you going to do when Arthur and I need time off for our wedding and honeymoon?"

"Did he pop the question?" The news yanked Harri out of her funk. Their IT guru was madly in love with Patty and adored Patty's daughter Grace. He may be a genius, but his self-esteem when it came to personal relationships could be precarious at best.

"Not yet, and don't you dare say a word to him." Patty narrowed her eyes. "He'll ask me when he's ready. Not before. And that's the point. I'm not letting my insecurities about abandonment run rampant when it comes to our relationship. Arthur loves me, and he shows me in a million ways Cade never could."

Harri took another sip of coffee to keep from making a sarcastic comment in response to her assistant's statement. Patty's ex-boyfriend, Cade Wilson AKA Black Death, had escaped from prison earlier this summer. Thankfully, Aisha's husband Rey, AKA Black Falcon, had captured the bastard. Cade was now in solitary confinement at Mauvaises Prison, the ultra-max facility for supervillains.

But this was the first time Patty had even mentioned Grace's biological father since he killed Arthur last year. Only Baby Grace had saved Arthur, and none of their immediate circle understood why or how Grace's powers had manifested that one time to bring Arthur back to life.

Even more worrisome was if Harri's goddaughter could kill like her father as well as heal. But if she brought up the subject, Patty would accuse her of deflecting from the more pertinent issues they were discussing.

"Anything else you need to lecture me about this morning?" Harri asked.

"Yes, apologize to both Aisha and Susan before they quit, and find that associate you promised us you would hire." Patty rose to her feet. "Now, Aisha and I have our own interviewing to do."

"Molly offered to watch the kids—" Harri started.

"She needs her own life," Patty snapped. "She's only twenty-three."

Not to mention, Molly Reinhold, AKA Nix, had been rather put out when Aisha insisted the girl go back to college and earn her degree instead of babysitting Mitch.

"So were you when Grace was born," Harri shot back.

"I am not having this argument with you." Patty pivoted on her sensible flats and marched out of Harri's office. Surprisingly, she closed the door gently behind her.

Harri sipped more of her coffee. What the hell was going on with everyone in the Law Office of Winters and Franklin? Did they expect her to be a figurehead? She was only looking for the most reasonable solutions to their problems, but everyone reacted like she was a tyrant.

She reached for the case file on the top of her inbox. Maybe the best way to deal with her irritation was to get some of her giant pile of work done before she left for Atlanta on Friday.

Or before she got more of an urge to test pointy, stabby things on her colleagues.

CHAPTER 3

In her own office, Aisha gestured for her interviewee to take a seat, and she settled on the couch opposite from him. Her foster brother Jeremy had obviously coached the young man. He was dressed in a navy suit, white dress shirt, and a matching navy and gold striped tie. His haircut would have cost more than the kid's rent, but she knew Jeremy or his husband Leonardo would have styled it for free. The young man was nervous, but not to the point his palms were super sweaty when he shook her hand. He perched on the edge of the second couch, his hands clasped and resting on his knees.

She smiled. "So, Mr. Keeler, tell me about yourself while we wait for Ms. Ames."

"Please, call me Dajon," he said.

"All right, Dajon."

"Well—" He cleared his throat. Phlegm made up for the lack of sweat. Maybe he should have taken Steve's offer for something to drink. "I have a Bachelor's degree in early childhood education. I worked for Early Bird Daycare while I was in school—"

Aisha waved a hand for him to stop. "No, I've read your resume. Tell me something else. Like what you do for fun."

"Um . . ." Dajon's skin was just light enough to turn a deep rose.

She laughed. "I grew up with Jeremy Harkness. If you met him through Lady Jaye's Revue, that's actually a point in your favor."

"Oh." Dajon released a deep breath. "Did he tell you about my last job?"

"If you mean the crazy mom who got you fired, yes, he did." She shook her head. "Parents can overreact when it comes to their kids."

"I swear I would *never* endanger any child in my care." Dajon signed a cross over his heart.

Aisha's office door opened, and Patty slipped inside. She had a soda in one hand and a bottle of water in the other. After setting the water in front of Dajon, she plopped onto the couch next to Aisha.

"It's not only the kids' safety we're worried about here, it's yours," Patty announced before she twisted the cap off her bottle.

"I beg your pardon?" His attention flipped from Patty to Aisha and back again.

Aisha glared at Patty. Sure, she needed to be involved in this decision because the daycare manager they hired would be watching both of their children. But she didn't need to scare any potential hire right out of the gate.

Patty shrugged. "He needs to understand what he's getting into." She turned back to Dajon. "Did Jeremy tell you what type of law firm we are?"

"Yes, ma'am." Dajon nodded. "He said you represented superheroes." He licked his lips. "But from what I've seen in the news, your firm has been doing a lot of criminal defense work lately."

Aisha resisted the urge to groan. However, Patty giggled.

"It's not by choice," Aisha said. "There were extenuating circumstances."

"I understand Ultramegaperson." Dajon cocked his head. "They're already a superhero client of yours who was wrongly accused. I'm talking about Miss Purrception and that attorney who tried to kill your partner, Ms. Winters."

"Again, there were extenuating circumstances," Aisha said.

"Are you expanding into criminal defense?" he asked.

"Whether we do or not, it has nothing to do with your position here."

"Yes, it does," Patty interjected. "He's going to be one of the lines of defense between our babies and the bad guys."

"Neither of you have any say in the clients we represent," Aisha said coolly. Dang it. She'd told Harri representing the supervillain was a big mistake even though Aisha owed Miss Purrception for helping out Aisha's husband Rey when Professor Paranoia kidnapped him and whisked him to Indonesia.

And the incident with fellow attorney Carol Inunza still left a bad taste in her mouth. Not just from Harri insisting they represent Carol after she helped Miss Purrception escape from prison, but putting Aisha in the position that she had to save her previous employer from plummeting to his death.

As Aisha feared, both incidents were causing problems, just not in the way she foretold to her partners.

Patty frowned at Aisha. "He has a right to ask about situations he might face in the workplace." She turned back to Dajon. "Those aren't even the people you need to worry about, though it's good you did your homework about a potential employer."

"They aren't?" Both of Dajon's perfectly plucked eyebrows rose.

"Nope." Patty shook her head, her blond curls flying. "Actually, it's the kids who live in the building."

"I'm surprised you didn't say it was the attorneys," Aisha said dryly.

Patty ignored her. "You'll be taking care of my daughter Grace, and Aisha's son Mitch, except during college breaks when you'll have Francisco to watch, too."

"Why would I be watching a guy old enough to go to college?" Dajon looked totally perplexed.

"Francisco is only eight," Aisha clarified. "He's our building manager's son and a certified genius. He finished high school last year, and he's attending college with his oldest brother."

"Oh." Relief passed across Dajon's face. "That makes a lot more sense."

"You will also be required to sign a non-disclosure agreement," Aisha added.

Dajon waved both of his hands. "I'd never post anything regarding your children on social media. I'm all too aware of the pervs out there."

Aisha tilted her head. "Actually, it's because you may accidentally run into clients, but it's reassuring to know you'll protect our babies."

"You'll also need to take some weapons training," Patty said.

Aisha looked over at their assistant's notepad. She really should have gone over Patty's interview questions with her prior to their first potential candidate. Patty was usually so practical, but some of her statements would sound crazy to a person who'd never been involved in real super culture, and not the crap they saw through various entertainment media.

"Weapons training?" Once again, Dajon's eyebrows rose.

"Just in case a supervillain or some other miscreant shows up when no one else is in the building," Patty chirped. "We'll totally brief you on all the building's security measures."

"Supervillains waltz right into your office?" A tremor filled Dajon's voice.

"They've tried," Aisha bit out. "Your priority if security is breached will be to get the kids to safety. Just like if there was a fire, an earthquake, or any other emergency situation."

The young man leaned back against the couch. "Jeremy said you all would have some crazy requirements, but I was sure he was yanking my chain."

A sinking feeling dragged at Aisha. They were losing this kid though he was the best candidate she'd talked to on the phone.

"They're not that unusual," she said smoothly.

"Unless Grace's biological father shows up," Patty said.

"Is it a joint custody arrangement?" he asked.

Patty snorted. "Not after he killed my boyfriend Arthur and tried to kill Harri. The judge gave me a restraining order after that."

"Your ex killed your boyfriend?" The stink of fear rolled off Dajon. Aisha wished she could ditch her heightened sense of smell. It was bad enough she knew when Mitch soiled his diaper before he even woke up.

"There's a little more to the story than that," she said calmly.

"I'm sure there is," he said with an air of doubt.

"I know how insane this all sounds." Patty leaned forward, her elbows on her knees. "I didn't really understand what superheroes go through until Harri and Aisha started this firm. But they're dedicated to their clients and their staff, and they do right by both."

"So . . ." Dajon drawled. "My real job is to give my charges a sense of normalcy out of their parents' crazy lives."

Aisha and Patty looked at each other before they both turned back to their candidate and nodded.

"That pretty much sums it up," Aisha added.

"I can do that." Dajon grinned.

"Did you have any other questions for us?" Aisha said.

He turned solemn. "I do have several, but the first one comes from a safety concern. Are either of the babies supers themselves?" He held up both of his palms when Aisha opened her mouth. "I'm not being nosey for the sake of gossip, and I understand this needs to stay quiet even before I sign your NDA. I just don't want one of the babies to set fire to the other one." He shrugged. "Or if there's the potential, we make sure there's plenty of fire extinguishers in the daycare room."

Aisha could feel Patty staring at her. She swallowed hard before she said. "Yes, they both are, but so far only one has displayed any super ability."

Dajon nodded. "I swear that information will not leave this building, ma'am. Jeremy also mentioned you may be expanding the daycare down the road?"

Aisha nodded. "We're looking for an associate or two. We want to make the daycare an option to any potential employees."

"Even me?" Dajon said tentatively.

"Of course," Patty volunteered. "But just to warn you, everyone at Winters and Franklin is a little too involved in each others' lives. How are your parents going to handle spending holidays with us?"

"Uh, my parents kicked me to the curb when I came out of the closet," he said stiffly.

Aisha stifled the urge to hug Dajon. No wonder Jeremy took the kid under his wing. Her parents had taken in Jeremy after his parents did the same thing to him when they caught him kissing his boyfriend their freshmen year in high school.

"Then we'll be the insufferable family you wish you had," Patty said brightly.

That seemed to lighten his mood. "Did you have any other questions for me?"

"You never said what you do for fun," Aisha said.

He lifted his chin as if daring her to make a nasty comment. "I crochet while I watch TV."

"That's awesome! Me, too!" Patty said. "I'm still learning the shell stitch. I've been working on blankets for all the kids, but I want to stretch . . ."

Aisha's mind glazed over as Patty and Dajon compared lemons and primroses and puffs. Then they switched to the different types of yarns. Natural fiber versus artificial fiber. Plant versus animal. The different types of hooks. Metal versus wooden versus plastic.

"If you two want to continue your conversation, why don't you adjourn to the conference room?" Aisha cocked her head. "I've got a lot of work to do."

A horrified look appeared on Dajon's face. "I, um, I—"

Patty winced. "Sorry. I didn't mean to go off on a tangent. It's not like any of you gals here are into the same things I am."

Aisha smiled. "I didn't say you couldn't continue talking. Don't worry, Dajon. If I held people's hobbies against them, I would never be partners with Harri and Susan." She leaned forward and mock whispered, "They like golf."

He laughed. "Well, it is a white thing."

Patty stood. "Come on, Dajon. You and I are going to continue talking. She does have to make the money to pay our salaries."

He stood and held out his hand to Aisha. "If you decide I'm the right one for this job, I'd be honored to work for your firm, Ms. Franklin."

She rose and shook his hand. "Thank you for coming in, Dajon."

He followed Patty out of Aisha's office, the pair animatedly talking about a local craft shop.

Aisha shook her head while she crossed to her desk. She plopped on her office chair and reached for the file at the top of her to-do pile. Hopefully, Patty wouldn't make the kid an offer before talking with the partners. They still had three more people to interview.

On the other hand, Patty and Arthur may end up adopting Dajon, even though he was only a year younger than her from Patty's animated conversation with their potential nanny.

Aisha sighed as she perused the motion Patty had drafted for her. If she'd known she was going to develop HRSP during her pregnancy, she would have paid Miguel to soundproof her office because Patty and Dajon's conversation regarding crocheting was going to put her to sleep.

CHAPTER 4

<hr>

Harri's cell phone warbled and broke her concentration on the action figure licensing contract for Violet Daze she was reviewing. She checked the caller. Jeremy. Now, why wasn't he calling Aisha? She was the one interviewing the kid he recommended for the daycare manager position. She thumbed the answer icon.

"Hola! Que pasa?"

"We have got to break you of that British accent when you speak Spanish. It's positively annoying." There was none of the salon chatter in the background. Either Jeremy was at home, or he was working at his unofficial side hustle—designing supersuits for heroes.

"According to Aisha, you just heard my entire Spanish vocabulary." Harri pulled off her reading glasses and leaned back in her office chair.

"That's not true, sweetie. You know how to say 'margarita,'" he shot back.

Harri laughed. "Look, if you're calling just to chat, can it wait until after work hours? I've a shit ton of stuff to get done before we leave for Atlanta on Friday."

"Actually, this is work related." When Jeremy turned serious, it meant superhero business. "I know you guys haven't been taking too many new clients—"

"Try not any, Jaye," Harri interjected. "Did you not hear what I just said about a shit ton of work before Martin and Renata's wedding?"

"I think you guys need to meet my client." Jeremy sighed. "Great potential, but he needs a kick in the backside. Huge chip on his shoulder."

She groaned. "Look, I get you want to save the world, but I don't have—"

"Just talk to him, sweetie," Jeremy pleaded. "That's all I'm asking."

"You owe me dinner at La Churro's—"

"Done!" Jeremy yelled.

"—for an entire year," Harri finished.

"Bitch," he growled.

"Takes one to know one." Harri would have stuck out her tongue if he could see her.

"When can you see my guy?" Jeremy persisted.

She tapped the keys on her laptop to bring up her calendar. "Can he come in this afternoon at two? That's the only time I've got open until we get back from the wedding."

"What about Aisha and Susan?" Jeremy just had to push.

"They are just as swamped as I am," Harri snapped. "What part of we're not taking new clients do you not understand? I've already got my partners breathing down my neck because I haven't had two minutes to pee much less interview potential associates."

"Thanks, Harri," Jeremy said. "Let me know when you're ready to start collecting on La Churro's." The line abruptly went dead.

Probably because whoever Jeremy wanted to send to her was sitting with him.

Crap. Why did she agree to this? She'd planned to pick up her bridesmaid dress from the alterations shop this afternoon. And if she brought home work for the twentieth night in a row, Tim would have a conniption fit.

Around ten minutes after noon, the antique elevator creaked and groaned as it rose to the fifth floor of the Lechuza Building. Harri hated asking her boyfriend for favors, but the dress was a necessity. Even though, she wasn't quite sure why Renata asked her to be a bridesmaid, other than Martin's biological and foster sisters matched her four brothers as groomsmen. If Tim agreed to pick up the dress while she talked to Jeremy's potential client and she got up an extra half hour early for the rest of the week, then, and only then, she might be able to safely go to Atlanta for the wedding.

Whistling floated down the hallway from the open doorway of her loft as the car ground to a halt. Harri pulled both gates open and exited the elevator. Super conscious of the infant living on the same floor, she pushed the gates closed.

Mitch may not be crawling yet, but she expected him to start flying any day now.

The whistling mixed with baby gurgling and cooing. She entered her loft to find Tim dancing around the kitchen to a pop song with Mitch on his hip while making lunch. He looked much younger than his forty-nine years, even though silver highlighted his auburn hair. The cargo shorts, vintage hair band t-shirt, and bare feet helped.

For the first time, regret infiltrated her heart. Regret that she'd strung her ex-husband Eddie along over his desire to have kids. Regret she hadn't encountered adult Tim sooner in her life. A red-headed baby with Tim's sense of humor might have made her change her mind about having her own children.

However, spoiling her godchildren would have to do. Wallowing over what could have been was never her style. She leaned against the wall and watched the joy exhibited by her boyfriend and her godson.

Tim abruptly halted his whistling and dancing in mid-squirt of mustard on her ham and cheese sandwich. Mitch gently patted Tim's face in an effort to restart his entertainment. Tim tapped a control on his phone to halt the music.

"How long have you been standing there?" he said.

"Long enough you should have tased and hogtied me if I were a supervillain." Harri sauntered over and took Mitch from Tim. "The original Ghost Owl is slipping in his old age," she said in a sing-song voice to the baby. "You'd better develop your powers soon, kiddo. Your uncle Tim is going to need you." She looked up at her boyfriend. "By the way, why do you have him?"

Tim shrugged. "Molly got an emergency call from the NSB. I told her I'd watch the kids until she got back. When Patty poked her head in to collect Grace, she said you'd interviewed the first potential nanny."

"Not me." Harri grinned. "I'm leaving that to the professional moms."

Mitch clapped his hands and laughed. She blew a raspberry on his round tummy, and he shrieked at the sensation.

"I'm assuming you and/or Arthur did background checks on all the applicants," she added.

"Arthur did, and Rey promised to pound the crap out of whoever takes the job if they screw up. So I'm leaving everything to the professional dads." For the first time in a long time, grief over the loss of Tim's own son didn't shadow his face.

"Crap, I was going to ask you for a favor." Harri grimaced.

"Something for the wedding?" Tim cocked his right eyebrow. "I think Mitch and I can handle it if you don't mind losing Arthur or Patty to Grace until we get back."

"Are you sure?"

He nodded.

"Can you pick up my bridesmaid dress from Hernandez Alterations?" she said. "They're on 10th Street."

"I can pick it up." Tim grinned. "And I know where it is. I think both our families have used them for a couple of generations."

"Thank you so much-ow!" She tried to gently pry Mitch's little fist from her ponytail.

"Ri-ri-ri!" he shrieked.

"I think he wants you to fly him around." Tim smirked as he turned to put away the condiments.

"Sorry, Mitch. Aunt Harri can't do it the same way as Mommy and Daddy." She winced as the kid's other hand latched onto her hair. He didn't need superstrength. His ability to yank on hair longer than Aisha's short afro could being anyone to tears. No wonder Rey broke down and let Jeremy trim his hair in a much shorter 'do. "Uh, Tim, I need a little help here."

Tim set aside the baby food jars he'd pulled from their cupboard and grabbed Mitch around his waist. "Wanna fly, little guy?"

Mitch shrieked again and released Harri's tresses. She blinked the tears out of her eyes while Tim made engine noises and zoomed their godson around the living room. After the second circuit, Tim landed Mitch in the spare high chair they kept in their loft. The baby giggled and clapped his hands some more.

"Can I ask why didn't you pick up your dress during lunch?" Tim asked as he buckled Mitch into his seat.

"First, I was hungry." Harri grabbed the jars of pureed lamb and green beans from the counter along with a baby spoon from the utensil drawer. "Second, it won't be ready until two. Third—" She steeled herself. "I've got a new client intake interview this afternoon."

Tim straightened. "Does this have anything to do with the huge fight you were having with Aisha and Susan first thing this morning?"

"You heard that?" Harri popped the seal on the jar of lamb.

"Trust me, it didn't take superhearing." Tim grabbed their plates and brought them to the table. He returned to the kitchen to grab a couple of flavored seltzer waters from the refrigerator.

Harri tried to hide her grimace. Tim was determined to change her eating habits, not to mention her drinking ones, too. It was a good thing Jeremy owed her multiple trips to La Churro's. It would be the only way for her to get her weekly dose of cheese dip and margaritas.

"If you keep making that face when I make lunch for you, Mitch will pick up your habits when his parents feed him," Tim chided.

"What face?" Harri dipped the baby spoon into the jar and offered a bite to Mitch. He gave the pureed lamb a suspicious look and clamped his mouth shut.

"You know the face," Tim lowered himself onto the chair on the other side of Mitch's high chair. "It's the same one you make when we go down to the gym first thing in the morning."

"Couldn't be the same expression. I hate exercising and love food." Harri crossed her eyes and stuck out her tongue. Mitch laughed, and she took the opportunity to insert the spoon between his lips. An expression of annoyance at her betrayal crossed his tiny features until the taste of lamb registered. He banged his tiny fists on the tray and opened his mouth wide, demanding more.

"But the seltzer water is better for you than soda," Tim said.

"You take away my coffee, and you won't have to worry about the faces I make." Despite her words, Harri smiled brightly at the baby as she spooned another bite of lamb between his tiny teeth.

"I'm not suicidal," Tim said dryly. "So, what made you change your mind about accepting a new client?"

"We haven't accepted them yet." She pushed the green beans in Tim's direction. "Would you open this?"

"What made you even want to talk to this person?" Tim twisted the lid, and the seal popped. "You swore you guys couldn't handle one more client until you hired an associate."

"Jeremy begged me." Harri dipped the spoon into the jar Tim slid back to her.

Tim snorted. "Since when has that started working?"

"It didn't." She inserted the spoon of pureed green beans in Mitch's open maw. If the kid ended up being the size of his dad, Aisha would need her extra income to feed her son. "The bribe is what made me change my mind."

"The bribe?" Tim groaned. "Let me guess. A dinner at La Churro's?"

"No." She dipped the spoon for another bite of lamb before she grinned at Tim. "It was dinners for a whole year."

"The plan was to get you healthy before you ended up like me," he growled.

"The plan was to keep supervillains from beating the crap out of you before the doctors have to do more than rebuild your leg and replace your knees." She scowled back at him. "And you're way too young for artificial joints."

"Do you really want to turn this into a fight, too?" he said quietly.

"I don't want to fight with anyone," she snapped back. "If you all would listen to reason—"

Tim abruptly stood. Even Mitch looked up at him with a perplexed look on his round face. "I'll eat in the lab. Bring Mitch down when he's done with his lunch." Tim grabbed his plate and stomped out of the loft.

Well, crap. She resisted the urge to run after him. She couldn't leave Mitch alone. Why the hell was everyone on edge when it was only Monday? It wasn't like anyone at the Lechuza building was getting married in two weeks.

Harri turned back to her godson. "Well, Mitch, I hope you're free for your uncle Martin's wedding. I may need a date."

Mitch stared at her with his big brown eyes before he belched.

CHAPTER 5

<hr>

Aisha walked out of her office to grab a soda as Tim charged into the reception area from the staircase, carrying a sandwich on a plate and a dark scowl on his face. She didn't have to ask who caused the latter or why he took the stairs instead of the elevator.

"What did she do this time?" she asked.

Patty twirled around on her chair to watch the fireworks.

"It's nothing," he muttered. But he stopped in front of the door to the basement and turned back to Aisha. "Why does she think she can run everyone's life?"

Aisha and Patty exchanged looks before they both looked at Tim again.

"I'll get the stash." Patty jumped up from her chair and headed for Arthur's office.

"What do you want to drink?" Aisha asked.

Tim blinked. "Drink?"

"You know . . ." She waved her hand in the direction of their break-room. "Coffee, tea, soda, water, milk, juice?"

His shoulders sagged. "Can I have water without anyone bitching at me about it?"

"Sure." She grinned. "Go have a seat in my office. We'll be there in a minute."

Aisha strode into the breakroom and collected a bottle of diet cola for herself and a bottle of water for Tim before she heated milk for Patty's hot chocolate. She carried all three drinks to her office. Patty ran in behind her and quietly closed the door.

"The phones?" Aisha asked.

"Aren't you the one who keeps telling me to let calls roll over to voicemail during my lunch hour?" Patty arched her right brow.

"Just don't let her catch you," Aisha muttered.

Tim's eyebrows rose when he caught sight of the boxes in Patty's hands. "Where'd you get Girl Scout Samoas this time of year?"

"You know the subzero freezer you have downstairs?" Patty grinned.

"I keep medical samples in that freezer!" Tim leaned away from the boxes she sat on the coffee table.

"Chill, Canyon." Aisha set Patty's mug on the table before she handed the bottle of water to Tim. "She's messing with you. We have a small chest freezer in Arthur's first floor workshop. It's the only cookie hiding place Harri hasn't found."

"Yet," Patty grumbled.

"So we'll share as long as you can keep your mouth shut," Aisha said. "Otherwise—"

"I'll chip in when you restock," Tim offered. "I didn't even get one cookie out of the three boxes I bought last spring."

"Exactly." Patty nodded as she ripped open the first package. "I learned my lesson back in our City Hall days. I made the mistake of sharing my Thin Mints. I started charging her. She'd pay me and inhale them just the same. But will she order them for herself?"

"No," Aisha said in sync with Tim.

"She did the same thing with me and Jeremy when we were undergrads," Aisha continued. "I thought it was some weirdness about not being able to afford them back then. Nope, she still did it when she interned for Judge Reeves. I thought his bailiff was going to kill her after she ate his four boxes of Tagalongs he stashed in his bottom desk drawer."

"I was hoping it was some crazy relationship thing." Tim took a couple of cookies out of the package Patty held out to him. "She does her best to drive me away, but when I accede to her wishes, she comes up with some new demand. I thought her weird push-pull behavior was why she ate all my cookies." He took a bite of one of the treats, ignoring the ham and Swiss sandwich on the plate in front of him.

"Don't take it personally." Aisha grabbed two cookies from the package Patty held out to her. "I think Jeremy and I are the only people in her life she hasn't driven away."

"That's not for lack of trying." Patty shoved a whole Samoa into her mouth and chewed loudly.

"Unfortunately, my life choices are probably what's driving her little trip to Crazytown today," Aisha admitted.

"There's no probably about it," Patty grumbled around her mouthful of cookie.

"Wait a minute." Tim cocked his head. "Where's Grace?"

Patty swallowed her cookie. "Arthur took her to the electronics supply warehouse with him and planned to get her chicken nuggets for lunch. It's not the park, but it gets her out of the building. And nice try in changing the subject."

Someone knocked, and they all froze with guilty expressions on their faces.

"I didn't lock the door," Patty whispered.

The knob turned, and the door swung open. Susan wore a puzzled expression until she spotted the two boxes on Aisha's coffee table.

"You bitches," Susan hissed before she closed and locked the office door. "I can't believe you dug into the stash without me." She laid the paperwork she carried on Aisha's office chair and grabbed the seat on the couch next to Tim. "Gimme."

Patty slid the open package across the table.

"Are we dishing about the battle royale this morning?" Susan grabbed a cookie and took a bite.

"Sort of," Aisha admitted. "Now she's taking her pissy mood out on Tim."

"This is getting ridiculous," Susan mumbled around the chocolate, caramel, and coconut. "She can't force you to stay in the United States while your husband is in France."

Tim shook his head. "I'm still trying to figure out why you agreed to taking on a new client when you're overloaded already."

"What new client?" Aisha's back and neck tensed. Not even her superpowers kept her muscles from contracting due to stress. Unfortunately, she could no longer go to her regular masseuse for any relief.

"Shit." Tim closed his eyes. "I didn't mean to spring this on you."

Susan stared at Aisha. "Is she deliberately trying to tank the firm?"

"The sad part is I don't think it's deliberate." Aisha shook her head. "Damn, every time I think she's gotten this insecurity crap out of her system, it blows up in my face."

"I can't be looking for a new job right now," Patty wailed. "Grace isn't ready for preschool yet."

"That's assuming you can ever send her." Aisha sank back in her couch and rubbed her forehead. "This is getting freakin' ridiculous."

"Can I amend my statement, counselor?" Tim wore a rueful grin. "In all fairness, she only agreed to talk to this person because Jeremy begged her."

She groaned. "No, it does not make me feel better. Jeremy knows how overwhelmed we are. At least, Patty and I are handling the daycare. I don't think she's made one damn call to find us an associate we can train."

"Why don't I stay in Canyon Pointe?" Susan offered. Again. "I'm not related to Martin like you and Harri are. I can start the associate search and weed out the unacceptable candidates before you guys get back from Atlanta."

"Maybe I should stay here with Susan. It's not like I'm family either." Patty nibbled on her lower lip.

"That's just exchanging one crabby woman for another." Aisha smiled. "I'll never hear the end of it from Aunt Queenie if you, Arthur, and Grace don't come."

"You mean, if Grace doesn't attend the wedding." Patty made a face.

"She's looking forward to spoiling both of our babies along with LaShun's kids. And she can throw a hissy fit to rival one of Harri's. Please don't make me suffer through both of them at the same time." Aisha popped the Samoa she'd been holding in her mouth and licked the melted chocolate smears from her fingers.

"I'm sorry she's still giving you crap about the Paris thing," Tim said. "I think it's a great idea for Rey to take the business courses in addition to the cooking ones. Not to mention exposing Mitch to the French language."

"Any ideas how to get her off my case?" Aisha said.

The bark of laughter from Tim held a bit of bitterness. "I can't get her off my case about the knee replacement surgery."

Aisha popped another cookie in her mouth. She was definitely going to need to raid the secret stash in order to survive this entire damn wedding trip.

CHAPTER 6

Harri carried Mitch down with her on the elevator. She didn't think the Owl's Nest was the best place for either Mitch or Grace to hang out, anymore than it had been for Francisco, but a year later, Miguel's youngest was attending one of the top STEM universities on a full scholarship. Arthur and Tim kept a playpen down there with an array of toys for the kids, along with diapers, bottles, and snacks. However, taking Mitch down to the Nest also meant she'd have to apologize to Tim even if she hadn't done anything wrong.

So she got off on the first floor to grab a bottle of plain water to call a truce. She entered the reception area as Aisha walked out of her office.

"What are you doing with my son?" her partner demanded.

"I fed him since the guy who was supposed to do it stormed out of my loft." Harri held out Mitch to Aisha. "I also burped him and changed his diaper."

Aisha frowned and didn't take her baby. "Molly's not back yet?"

"Does it look like she's back?"

Instead of taking Mitch, Aisha pulled out her phone and started scrolling with her thumb. "Well, crap. It looks like one of the cables holding the shipping containers in place either wasn't secured properly or snapped. Nix is using ultrasonics to keep the ship stable while Black Falcon and Captain Mojave are retrieving the containers."

She looked up at Harri. "You know the shipping company is going to try to blame the supers. I guess I need some more coffee and have Arthur pull surveillance footage for me when he gets back from his errand." She pivoted and took a step toward the break room.

"Hey, what about your son?" Harri snapped.

"Well, you weren't bringing him to me, were you?" Aisha pointedly looked at her office door, then at the door to the basement. "If I were you, I'd do some serious sucking up to my man."

"I didn't do anything!" Harri glared at her partner.

Aisha slid her phone back into her slacks pocket. "Taking your anger at me out on Tim isn't helping your relationship either. He said he'd watch Mitch until Molly gets back. Since you chased him down to the Nest, you need to be the one to take Mitch down there and apologize."

Harri gritted her teeth, but she wasn't going to win this one. Aisha could be more stubborn than Captain Mojave. Maybe that was why their friendship survived when all Harri's other relationships bit the dust.

Aisha took two more steps toward the break room before she pivoted on her stilettos to face Harri again. "By the way, I do not want to hear any more bitching from you about me going to Paris if you are going behind my back to recruit more clients." She flew to the break room, probably to keep from breaking her precious designer shoes by stomping on the antique floor tiles.

Or breaking the irreplaceable art deco tiles with her superstrength.

Blood roared in Harri's ears. Dammit! Tim narced on her! She didn't need this crap from either her boyfriend or her law partner. She was definitely calling Jeremy and collecting on one of the dinners he owed her tonight.

❧

None of the Owl's Nest security measures were active when Harri and Mitch reached the bottom of the basement stairs. Technically, the superhero lair belonged to Tim as the original Ghost Owl, but Rey and Aisha had sort of inherited it. Or rather, their superhero personas Black Falcon and Ghost Owl II had inherited the hideout.

Actually, a good chunk of the superheroes in Canyon Pointe used the Owl's Nest at times. All of them happened to be Winters and Franklin clients, too.

Like Molly Reinhold AKA Nix.

Lights flickered on as the motion sensors picked up Harri's strides. Mitch nestled against her shoulder and chest. He was about ready to pass out for his post-lunch nap. She prayed Tim wasn't running any heavy machinery. Mitch without his nap could be as cranky as his mom without pixie barf first thing in the morning.

When she entered the lab, Tim quietly clicked away on his ergonomic keyboard. Yet another concession he'd made for her, she realized with a pang of guilt. They'd both gotten the same model when they'd spent one evening icing their wrists after a particularly intense round of video games with the Esperanza boys over the summer.

He looked up at her, and the cold anger from earlier still sparked from his dark blue eyes.

"I came down to apologize. I'm sorry for taking my anger with Aisha out on you. It wasn't fair." She forced the words between her teeth. "Can you please still watch Mitch while she and I meet with Jeremy's potential client?"

Tim's face softened a bit. "Thank you for apologizing. And yes, I'll watch *our* godson and pick up your bridesmaid dress."

"You don't have to—"

"I said I would, and I will," he stated firmly. "I'm not that petty." He stood and held out his hands for the baby. "Though I will wait until after his nap."

Mitch barely opened his eyes at the trade-off. He made sucking noises with his pacifier, and his eyes drifted shut again. Tim laid Mitch in the portable bassinet next to his computer desk. The pacifier fell out of the baby's mouth, and he was softly snoring before Tim could lay the Black Falcon baby blanket over Mitch.

Yep, Aisha definitely had more of a clue of marketing and licensing superhero merchandise than Harri did.

"What are you working on?" Harri asked.

"Finishing up the background check on your afternoon appointment," Tim murmured.

"But Arthur—"

"Had to run an errand, and he took Grace with him." Tim straightened. "Remember?"

"Does this have anything to do with a ring?" Harri raised an eyebrow.

A funny look came over Tim.

"Oh, my god!" Harri resorted to waving her hands excitedly to keep herself from yelling and waking Mitch. "When's he going to ask her?"

"I'm staying out of Arthur and Patty's business." Tim crossed his arms over his chest. "And you are, too."

"You're no fun." Harri wrapped her arms around his waist. "Bet I could convince you to tell me."

"You can try, but don't you have a client intake interview in an hour?"

"Getting too old for a lunchtime quickie?" she mocked.

"I prefer to take my time and make sure things are done right." Tim unfolded his arms, cupped her head, and lowered his lips to hers.

Their kiss was slow. And sweet. Really sweet. She detected hints of chocolate, caramel, coconut and vanilla cookie in his taste.

Harri broke the kiss and glared at Tim. "Where did you get the Samoas?"

CHAPTER 7

The intercom buzzed. Aisha glanced at her phone set. Instead of Patty or Susan, it was Harri.

Harri who would usually barge into Aisha's office if she wanted to discuss something and never, ever used the intercom. As tempting as it was to ignore the machine, Aisha gently poked the correct button. No sense in putting her entire fist through the set.

Even if it was accidentally. She'd destroyed enough furniture and equipment thanks to her superpowers.

"Yes?"

"Jeremy's referral is here," Harri said coolly. "Would you like to do the intake interview in my office, yours, or the conference room?"

Harri never shared the intake interview duties either. Thankfully, her attitude had only caused a problem once, and when she realized it was a set-up by their rival firm Dewey and Cheatham, she chewed Quantum Commander a new one.

Between Jeremy and Aisha working the superhero gossip vine, Quantum Commander lost most of his endorsements. Dewey and Cheatham dropped him soon afterward. Served the asshole right for getting in bed with those psychopathic con artists. A part of Aisha still wished she'd let Howard Dewey splatter all over pavement when he tripped over Cobblestone, whom Howard had just shot, and tumbled out of his corner office's huge picture window.

"We can do it in your office," Aisha said pleasantly. Sure, the room was Harri's territory, but it gave Aisha an excuse to leave if she needed to do so. "I'll be right there."

She grabbed a legal pad and a pencil. Pens had been a no-no for the last year and a half thanks to her superstrength first from hormone-related superpowers, known colloquially as HRSP, while she was pregnant. Then her mother-in-law Xquic, the Mayan goddess, made her powers permanent.

Aisha strode out of her office. Patty frowned, so Aisha raised an eyebrow. Their assistant shrugged.

So, Patty wasn't sure why Harri was acting solicitous either.

Aisha crossed the reception area and knocked on Harri's door before she opened it. A man, who had been sitting on the couch against the window, stood. A zillion tiny braids tamed his black curls. A neat circle beard framed his generous mouth. He dressed in a conservative style suit, but the color was a deep purple. His eyes were what captured the majority of her attention. His irises were so dark she couldn't tell where they ended and the pupils began.

"Come on in," Harri said a little more congenially than when she was on the intercom a moment ago. "Aisha Franklin, this is Shadowstar. Shadowstar, my legal partner Aisha Franklin. I'll be the first to admit she's the brains behind our law firm."

Shadowstar. The name wasn't familiar, but he could be new, or he simply needed a rebrand like Nix had and had already chosen a new moniker.

The superhero flashed very white teeth in his smile. "I've heard a lot of great things about y'all, but I also heard you weren't taking new clients. I was a little surprised when Jeremy said he had an in with you ladies." Shadowstar had the slightest hint of a Georgian drawl.

"He also begged Harri because he knew I would have kicked his ass for promising something without checking with us first." Aisha gestured at the couch. "Have a seat, Mr. Shadowstar."

Once they were settled on the couches, or in Aisha's case the matching arm chair, Harri said, "I explained to Shadowstar this was simply an interview to see if our working styles were compatible, not a guarantee of representation."

It took everything Aisha had to keep her expression neutral. Harri never sucked up like this no matter what she had done or how much she irritated Aisha. What the hell was going on now?

But Aisha couldn't interrupt this meeting to ask. Not for the first time, she wished she could trade in her supersenses for telepathy. That way she'd know what the hell was going on in the morass that passed for Harri's brain.

"Do you mind if I ask how y'all know Mr. Harkness?" Shadowstar asked. "I got the impression it was more than a professional relationship."

"We all met in grade school a long time ago." Aisha chuckled. "But he wouldn't have taken you on as a client, much less pushed us to consider you for our firm's representation, unless he thought you had what it took to be a successful superhero."

"And what exactly is that, Ms. Franklin?" Shadowstar flashed another brilliant white smile.

She recognized the flirty behavior, but Shadowstar's genial charm more than compensated for any creepiness the same behavior Stuart Cheatham exuded at her previous employer's. Mom said never to speak ill of the dead, but Stuart got what he deserved.

"First of all, listening to your attorneys," she said more sharply than she intended. "If you visited with Jeremy, has he put together some design concepts for your supersuit?"

"Yes, ma'am," he said.

"Do you consent to us doing a background check on you?" Harri said.

Shadowstar hesitated. "That depends on whether you hold someone's past against them, Ms. Winters."

"It's better that you're upfront with us now," Aisha said.

"But you two don't expect me to hold the fact you've represented supervillains in the past against you?" he said with a scowl.

"It sounds like you did your homework," Harri said. "Why would you want to be represented by a law firm that has represented supervillains?"

He opened his mouth, caught himself, and chuckled. "Touché, Ms. Winters."

"And I've noticed you haven't answered any of my partner's questions," Aisha said.

"All right." He held up his palms. "No, I don't care if you do a background check. I have a juvenile record. Grand theft auto at age twelve. The only reason I'm free is because I was tried and convicted as a juvenile and aged out of the system."

"And after that?" Harri prompted.

He obviously didn't like her asking the questions. "I tried to go straight. When I was in the system, I discovered I had powers. The irony is my powers let me hide from the government."

"What do you mean you *tried* to go straight?" Aisha pursed her lips. This guy was definitely dancing around the issues.

"I worked at a pizza joint," he said. "An armed gunman came in to rob the place. He shot my manager to prove he was serious. I used my powers to disarm the gunman, but no one caught on. The cops and the owner all decided I was in on the attempted robbery. The idiot gunman's family sued me and the owner for assault. And then I was fired."

"But you weren't charged with criminal assault, correct?" Harri asked.

"No, just misdemeanor public disturbance." Shadowstar grimaced. "But because of that, I haven't been able to keep a job since then."

"Why?" Harri waved her hand. "You can tell them the truth without saying anything about how you took down the robber—"

"He means he has been lying by omission." Aisha glared at him. "He's not telling potential employers about the disturbance charge, so when they do find out, the employers feel doubly betrayed."

"You sound like my sister." A wry smile crossed his face.

"Maybe you should listen to her," Aisha said dryly. "Or are you one of those people who thinks becoming a superhero will magically solve your money and employment problems?"

His chin jutted forward. "It could if I had the right team."

"We require our clients to follow a certain set of rules to ensure their success." Aisha glared at him.

"Rules?" Anger flashed in his eyes. "Like 'Yes, Miss Daisy'. 'Anything you say, Miss Daisy'?"

"It's not rules exactly," Harri interjected. "It's more like suggestions to ensure your success—"

"So I've got to play the good little house boy for a bunch of rich women?"

What the hell was going on here? The firm was already overloaded. Why was Harri trying to smooth things over with this jerk when he obviously didn't care about how the public perceived him? This wasn't a race issue. It was a PR issue. If he didn't get that now . . .

Though Aisha seethed at Shadowstar's attitude, she plastered on her gracious smile and stood. "I have another meeting to attend. My partner can continue discussing our . . . suggestions with you. Thank you for considering Winters and Franklin for your legal needs."

She stalked out of Harri's office before she did anything stupid.

Like punching the jerk through a stone wall.

She was halfway across the reception area when he called out, "Ms. Franklin, wait!"

Aisha forced her shoulder muscles to relax and plastered the damn smile back on her face before she turned to face the super. "Yes?"

"I'm really sorry for upsetting you." He stopped with his palms raised slightly. A pleading gesture. "I expected difficult questions about my past from Ms. Winters. I assumed you would be more sympathetic to my situation."

"Because I'm a sister?" she bit out. In her peripheral vision, Patty's mouth hung open at the confrontation. Of course, their assistant was shocked. Aisha was always the one soothing feathers Harri ruffled.

"Well, yeah." He shrugged.

"My parents are both professionals. Neither of Harri's had college degrees." She let her face twist into a scowl. "Harri's parents were drug addicts. Mine weren't. Harri ended up in the foster system. I didn't."

He frowned. "So, what? You're proud to be an oreo?"

Aisha stepped closer to Shadowstar. "Don't ever call me that again."

"Or what?" He grinned.

"I can see why you failed before." Aisha shook her head. "You need to stick everyone in your neat little labeled boxes. That's not reality."

His smile faded. "Or maybe I was the one who people stuck their label on," he growled.

"If everything is everyone else's fault, you're never going to make it as a superhero." She turned to walk away.

That's when he made the mistake of grabbing her arm.

All the day's pent up anger rushed out. She twisted out of his hold and shoved him. He flew backwards into the wall beside Harri's office door.

But instead of hitting the stone, Shadowstar disappeared into it.

CHAPTER 8

—◆◆◆—

Harri reached her office doorway in time to see Shadowstar shoot straight into the wall on her right.

And phase right through the stone and plaster to land unceremoniously on the couch she'd just vacated.

She turned back to her partner. "What the fuck, Aisha!"

"Well, damn," Shadowstar muttered behind Harri. She turned back to him, and he roared with laughter.

"Are you all right?" Harri approached him. "I swear she doesn't do things like this during other intake interviews."

He grinned and sat upright. "Jeremy didn't tell me y'all were literally super attorneys."

From heels clicking behind Harri, Aisha approached her office. Harri whirled around, marched back to the entrance and mouthed, "No," before she shut her office door in her partner's face. Not that it would make any difference with Aisha's superhearing, but someone needed to smooth things over with Shadowstar. If Aisha was going to start a brawl—

Harri inhaled deeply and released the air. She never would have believed that last thought would have ever entered her mind. Everyone accused her of acting crazy. Aisha would be lucky if Shadowstar didn't file assault charges on her for shoving him into, or rather through a wall. Harri turned around to face their potential client.

• 42 •

He stood and straightened his clothes. "I guess I owe you an apology, too, Ms. Winters. I made a lot of assumptions I shouldn't have. Thank you for your time." He strode toward the door, a disappointed look on his face.

"So, that's it?" she said. "You're just going to run away like you have every other time?"

Shadowstar paused with his hand on the antique cut glass door knob, but he wouldn't meet her gaze. "You know nothing about me."

"I know what it's like trying to run away from the pain," Harri murmured. "Except the pain is inside, so you will always take it with you. You've got to face it eventually. Otherwise it's going to eat you alive."

"Things don't change for people like me." He continued to stare at the floor.

"They can." She cocked her head. "That's assuming you really want to become a superhero."

"I want my son to be proud of me." He looked at her. "You're the heir to the Winters' fortune. Why are you being nice to me?"

She laughed. Over the years, that assumption had become a source of amusement, instead of anger and embarrassment. Or that's what she told herself to keep from weeping over her real losses. "Shadowstar, the Winters fortune consisted of a couple of kilos of cocaine and a Porsche, both of which went over a cliff with my dad and stepmonster. Aisha wasn't bullshitting you. Both Jeremy and I ended up in the system. Where's your son?"

A frown tugged at the corners of Shadowstar's mouth, giving her all the answer she needed. "When was the last time you saw him?"

The muscles along his jaws clenched. She didn't think he was going to answer her until he murmured, "When he was three days old. He was premature. The social worker got a court order to take him away from my girlfriend and me." He sagged against the door. "That was five years ago."

"I take it you and your girlfriend aren't together any more," Harri said gently.

He shook his head. "She's married now. Got a kid with her husband."

"Have either of you tried to get back custody of your son?"

"I can't get anywhere without a job." He shrugged again, but the pain in his expression was brutal. Raw. He had been screwed over for doing the right thing like everyone else here in the Lechuza Building.

"Do you want to continue the intake interview?" Harri gestured at the couches by the front window. "We can reschedule if you don't feel up to it. Or I can give you a referral to another firm that specializes in superhero representation, given my partner's poor behavior."

He cocked his head. "You don't seem like the typical white savior."

She laughed again. "Everyone who works here has their own damage, no matter what color their skin is."

"So what's Ms. Franklin's problem? Other than she's a super." He had the usual male interest in her partner.

"One, that's for her to tell, not me." Harri propped her fists on her hips. "Two, you'd better notice that wedding ring on her finger because I'm not responsible for you doing another stupid stunt like touching her without permission."

"Is that one of the rules I have to abide by?" A mischievous twinkle shone in Shadowstar's dark eyes.

"Unless you want your balls electrocuted or your brain turned to gelatin, keep your hands to yourself," she said sternly. "None of the attorneys, the staff, or our clients put up with shit. We're literally family here, and that's not some BS motto. We're very careful about who we accept into our fold, and we watch each others' backs."

"Understood." He nodded. "I'd like to continue with the interview if you don't mind."

"All right." She gestured at the couches. "But remember, all the partners have a say in taking you on as a client, and you've already pissed off one of them."

"Then I'll have to rectify Ms. Franklin's opinion of me."

Harri refrained from commenting. If the idiot didn't get his act together, he'd have more trouble than simply irritating the Ghost Owl.

Once the other clients got done with Shadowstar, there wouldn't be enough left of him to bury.

Chapter 9

—◆●◆—

Once Patty buzzed Aisha to let her know Shadowstar had left and Harri was safely ensconced in her own office with her door shut, Aisha took her laptop and retreated to her loft. It was bad enough she'd lost her temper with that conceited super wannabe and revealed her own powers. Part of her wanted to follow through and beat the crap out of Shadowstar.

She headed back to the bedroom to change into something more comfortable than her slacks and blouse. Her phone buzzed as she yanked her t-shirt over her head. She checked the device. Rey texted he would be late since Reuben covered his shift at the restaurant while he and the other superheroes dealt with the disabled ship and its cargo issues on Lake Del Oro. At least, her husband promised to bring supper home with him. She responded before she slid her phone in her shorts pocket. Rey was definitely the best thing that ever happened to her.

Aisha padded into the kitchen in her bare feet to scrounge a snack to tide her over and something cold to drink. Today had to be the crappiest Monday on record.

A twinge of guilt rang through her. She was damn lucky she hadn't hurt Shadowstar no matter how much he had annoyed her. And now, she'd given Harri a real reason to be angry with her. Hell, it sucked to admit it, but if Jeremy had called Aisha about this guy first, she would have given in to his pleading, too.

Her phone rang as she mixed cashews and cheddar crackers in a bowl. She pulled it out of her pocket and glanced at the caller ID. Renata.

She closed her eyes. Dammit, the stupid wedding was the last thing she wanted to talk about, but her future sister-in-law wouldn't call unless it was important. Renata didn't need Aisha to be spilling her crappy mood all over the place when the poor woman was already stressed to the max.

Aisha thumbed the answer icon and tried to put a positive note in her voice. "Hey, girl! What's up?"

"Why didn't you tell me you and Rey are moving to Paris?" Renata's shriek made Aisha hold the phone away from her ear.

"Superhearing, Renata."

She lowered her volume. "Oops. Sorry about that. I keep forgetting."

Aisha laughed for the first time today. "It's all right, girl. Sometimes, I forget myself. I've had to replace nearly everything I own over the last year and a half. Who let the news slip?"

"Aunt Queenie," Renata said with a giggle. "I think she's a little jealous."

Aisha snorted as she padded to the fridge. "I think my great-aunt would have a Rey and Steve sandwich if she thought Qiang and I would let her get away with it."

"That's the truth," Renata said. Her laughter died. "I hate to ask, but I need a little help with something."

"You said you didn't want a bridal shower," Aisha teased while she examined the contents in her refrigerator. No wonder Rey was bringing home dinner. The appliance was practically empty except for soft drinks and formula. She selected one of Rey's orange sodas from Mexico. The kind with real sugar in a glass bottle. "You can't renege now."

"Actually, that's the problem." Renata sighed. "Your mom's decided I have to have one, and not even Aunt Queenie has been able to talk her out of it."

"How is she planning to squeeze it in?" Aisha flicked off the bottle cap with her thumbnail. "The wedding is a week from Saturday."

"I'm very aware of the date of my wedding," Renata said sourly. "I wish I'd tried harder to convince Martin to go to Vegas."

"Oh, you were never going to do that, girl." Aisha took a swig of soda. "He's the one who wanted the fancy church wedding when we were kids."

"I liked yours and Rey's idea of a simple ceremony followed by a neighborhood party."

Aisha laughed. "I'd tell you to change arrangements—"

"But it would be a toss-up between Martin throwing a temper tantrum for not having his special day, or all the parents throwing a fit about the money," Renata grumbled.

"Wait a minute." Aisha slid onto one of the kitchen bar stools and pulled her bowl of crackers and nuts closer. "I thought you and Martin were paying for your own wedding."

"We are. Doesn't stop everyone in both families from bitching about something." Renata made a funny sound somewhere between a laugh and a sob. "You mom wants to have the shower the Saturday before the wedding. I'm still trying to wrap up things at my office, and I've got a zillion errands I have to run."

"Don't worry, girl," Aisha said. "I'll take care of the shower problem."

"Please don't be mean to your mom," Renata said.

"I won't." Aisha chuckled. "I'll sic Lady Jaye on her. She owes me anyway."

As soon as Aisha finished talking to Renata about a couple other wedding matters, she tapped the speed dial icon for Jeremy.

"Ish bedder be 'ood, Aisha," Jeremy mumbled. "I'n in dee middle uh soneding."

"Please tell me that's not Leo's dick in your mouth," she retorted.

There were several metallic *clink*s in the background. "Wash out your mouth with soap for speaking about my husband that way. Seriously, I'm still working on my baby doll's suit for the wedding. Can this wait?"

"No, it can't. Not to mention you owe me for pushing a new client on Harri right before we're supposed to fly to Atlanta," Aisha growled. "She's already crawling up my butt about moving to Paris for a year."

"Oh, dear," he murmured. "All I asked for was an intake interview. I didn't expect you to do any work before the wedding—"

"Just stop, Jeremy. Please." She held the cold bottle against her forehead. "We've got other problems. Do you know Mom wants to push a bridal shower on Renata?"

"Shower?" Jeremy slurped something thick and liquidy.

"Oh, my god, are you drinking those disgusting diet shakes again?" Aisha muttered.

"I don't have the luxury of your metabolism," he snapped, but he softened his voice. "I thought we were going with a relatively small and non-showery get together because Renata told LaShun she couldn't deal with anything else."

"She did." Aisha took a long swing of soda before she added. "Mom's on a tear, and not even Aunt Queenie can talk her down."

"Oh, geez." Jeremy groaned. "In other words, you want me to have a little chat with Betty."

"You are her favorite daughter." Aisha laughed. "If anyone can get through to her, it's you."

"Honey, you realize she's still pissed at me because Leo and I eloped last year?"

"We are all still pissed you two eloped." A pang twisted her heart even though she chuckled. At the time, everyone believed Rey was dead, and the guys honestly didn't want to hurt her by flaunting their happiness in her face. "However, you're the last resort to keep Renata from having a nervous breakdown before she says her own vows."

"I'll call Betty in a few minutes." He paused, and Aisha knew what was coming. "How did things go with Shadowstar? I told Harri to be careful with him."

"She was." Aisha took another swig of soda.

"Aisha?" Jeremy drawled. "What happened?"

"Between calling me an oreo and grabbing my arm, I lost my temper."

"Honey, the asshats at Dewey and Cheatham did worse for years, and you put up with their shit—"

"I pushed Shadowstar through a wall," she interrupted.

"Through a wall, or *through* a wall?"

"He phased before he hit the stone." Aisha popped a couple of crackers into her mouth. Just thinking about the jerk made her want to do something nasty to him for his conceited attitude. Chewing seemed her safest option for now.

"An-n-nd?" Jeremy prompted.

"I don't know," she said around the cheddar crackers. She swigged more soda. "I think he landed in Harri's office, but she slammed her door in my face so I don't know for sure."

"And the Ghost Owl didn't kick in the door and continue the beat down? Isn't that what you supers do to each other? Even when you're both good guys? Didn't you lose your condo thanks to Captain Justice and Cobblestone wrecking the place?" Jeremy's mocking tone drove home just how stupidly she had acted.

"All right, all right," she said. "I get your point."

"No, you don't, Aisha." It wasn't often Jeremy lost his temper, but he was definitely steamed. "You know damn well no other firm will touch him. Not with a juvenile criminal record. You had no problem hiring Arthur—"

"Arthur wasn't trying to become a superhero!" The tension in her shoulders and neck were back, and she turned her head back and forth to try to loosen the muscles. "All he wanted was some freaking attention for his talents!"

"I expect this sort of temper tantrum shit from Harri," Jeremy spat. "You know better."

Someone knocked on her loft door. Aisha took a deep breath and let it out. "Look, I've got to go. You can yell at me about Shadowstar another time. I'm asking for your help because Mom's driving Renata crazy, and you're the only other person Mom would listen to besides LaShun. This is for Renata, not me."

"All right, but you owe me," Jeremy warned. "I expect you to talk to Shadowstar again."

"Fine." Aisha slid from her stool and strode over to the loft door.

"Pinky swear," Jeremy threatened.

"I pinky swear. Get your man's threads done for our brother's damn wedding." She thumbed the end call button as she rolled back the door.

Tim entered with Mitch, who was out cold in Tim's chest harness. A quizzical eyebrow rose on the inventor's forehead. "Everything okay?" he murmured.

"Yeah." She carefully lifted her son from the baby carrier.

"Uh-huh. You realize Patty already tattled on you and Harri, right?"

He unhooked the harness while she cradled Mitch. "You gave me an ear earlier. I'd be happy to return the favor."

"It's nothing," Aisha muttered.

"Really?" He shook his head. "The Ghost Owl doesn't out herself by shoving a potential client through a wall."

She winced. "All right. Yes, I screwed up. Jeremy just chewed me a new one for it over the phone. I don't need it from you, too."

"I wasn't going to do that." Tim gestured at her sleeping son. "I'm actually worried some supervillain has swapped my girlfriend and her best friend's brains. You don't resort to violence, and you never did before you had powers either."

Aisha chuckled. "Ask Cobblestone what I did to him with one of Cal's golf clubs before my HRSP started."

"How about a trade, then?" Tim said. "I'll listen to your problems, and you give me some advice about mine."

"Is she still throwing your past in your face?"

"No, this is sort of a new one." Tim scowled.

"It's a deal." Aisha flew back to Mitch's room to keep from jarring him awake, but her heart ached. If Tim couldn't help her figure out a way to deal with Harri, she may not have a choice but to leave the firm.

CHAPTER 10

◆━━━━◆●◆━━━━◆

Harri finally walked out of her office well after Patty had quit for the day. She couldn't deal with anymore disappointed mom looks from their assistant. Everyone else's doors were closed, and their office lights were off. She should go up to her own loft since it was her turn to make dinner and tell Tim they were going out tonight, but she didn't want to take the chance of running into Aisha. She couldn't deal with her business partner right now.

Instead, she texted for a taxi before she sent a message to Tim to say she was meeting Jeremy for dinner at La Churro's, and he was welcome to join them. She waited between the twin sets of bulletproof glass doors. When the bright yellow cab pulled to a stop in front of the Lechuza Building, she raced out to the taxi with the need to escape the tension in her business and home.

"Hey, Dopinder!" she said brightly as she slid into the rear seat and yanked the door shut.

"Good evening, Miss Harri!" He pressed the button to start his taxi's meter running before he checked his mirrors and pulled into the remnants of rush hour traffic. "Are we picking up Black Falcon and Nix for a celebratory dinner after their rescue of the ship in Lake Del Oro, or are we meeting another client for a press conference?"

"Nope, it's a La Churro's night." She grinned at his reflection in the rearview mirror.

The driver groaned. "You're not planning to get sloshed again, are you? Really, Miss Harri, what kind of example are you setting for your clients?"

"I admit I'm not setting a good example for my godchildren, which is why I'm riding in a cab and not driving." She leaned her elbows on the front bench seat. "Have you heard of a super who calls himself Shadowstar?" Tim and Arthur couldn't find anything stored on a computer anywhere in the world, but she'd come to depend on Dopinder for any street rumors. It helped she kept him on a generous private retainer to pick up her clients in emergency situations.

He frowned. "Name doesn't ring a bell. What's his power set?"

"He can phase through solid objects," she replied.

"Doesn't sound like anyone I've heard of in Canyon Pointe." He glanced at her via the mirror. "I can check with my sources for the usual fee."

She laughed. "What's on your kids' want list?"

"Lalita wishes for the Sparx Power House and the hard-to-find alternate costume, Sanjay would like the new Cobblestone with the Power Punch, Kunal of course wants to attend Black Falcon's next public event, and Parvati would like the Ultramegaperson Glamor Kit."

"I think I can manage that, but can I deliver their fee in two weeks? I'm leaving town for my foster brother's wedding."

"Your parents took in foster children?" He shot her a quizzical look via the rearview mirror before returning his attention to traffic.

"Other way around. His parents took me in after my mom and dad died."

"My apologies, Miss Harri."

"Nothing to apologize for, Dopinder." She patted his shoulder before she sat back in her seat. He wasn't the first to assume the rich white family would take in the poor black children. Sadly, she couldn't see her father or the stepmonster taking in LaShun, Aisha, and Martin if something had happened to Marvin and Betty. Maybe Grandma Harri would have.

Or would she?

So many things Harri had believed about her grandmother turned out to be lies. Tim had been doing some quiet checking for her, but he hadn't found a damn thing regarding the list of people Grandma Harri had left in the storage unit for her. If they were children the government or Corvus had abducted from their parents, was Grandma Harri helping with the kidnapping? Or was she relocating the kids and their families to keep them out of Corvus's clutches?

As much as Harri wanted to believe it was the latter, she'd been an attorney and a Winters long enough to know things were never that simple.

Maybe that was the core of her issue with Aisha. She was afraid of being left out and burned if Aisha and Rey decided to stay in Paris after he graduated from the culinary school. Aisha had been more than a best friend. She kept Harri sane when child services took her away from the only home she'd ever known.

Thankfully, Dopinder wasn't the type of driver who felt the need to chatter for the entire ride. When she needed time to think, he remained blissfully silent unless he needed to say something.

"Here we are." He pulled up in front of La Churro's and rattled off the charge. She slipped her debit card into the machine and added a healthy tip.

Dopinder ducked his head to see her through the passenger window as she climbed out. "Call me if you need a ride home, Miss Harri. I've seen you and Mister Jeremy after a couple of pitchers of strawberry margaritas."

"I will." She grinned. "Have a good night!"

The little statue of Ganesh on Dopinder's dash bobbed its elephant head in agreement as the taxi drove off into the dusk.

Harri entered the Mexican restaurant. She spent a lot of time at La Churro's with Jeremy and Aisha through her law school years. Their food was decent and cheap, and the drinks weren't watered down. Jeremy waved at her from a booth.

However, when she walked over to that section of the restaurant, Leo sat next to his husband. "Hope you don't mind me tagging along."

"Of course not." She grinned while both men climbed out of the booth and hugged her. The guys resumed their seats, and she slid into the bench opposite of them.

"Timmy isn't coming?" Jeremy's right eyebrow rose as he poured orange slush into her glass.

"I don't know. He hasn't texted me back yet." She cocked her head. "That ain't no strawberry."

"It's mango margarita." Jeremy pushed the glass to her. "Mateo has been bringing different flavors to the post-revue parties for opinions before adding any to the menu."

"Leave it to the queens to pick out the party drinks." Leo raised his glass, and Harri clinked hers against his and then Jeremy's before she stuck the straw between her lips.

She took a sip and swirled the icy, tart liquid around her mouth before she swallowed. "That is excellent! He needs to keep it on the menu." She reached for the basket of tortilla chips and popped one in her mouth.

"When are you coming to see the new show?" Leo asked with a faux innocent air.

Jeremy nudged Leo with his shoulder. "Don't go there."

"It's been over a year since either she or Aisha has come to Lady Jaye's Revue." Leo pouted. His blue cowlick added to the bad boy sullen expression. "How much longer are you two going to punish us for eloping?"

"This isn't about you two getting married." Harri sucked down another mouthful of mango margarita. "Without inviting either family, I might add. We're overworked to the point I have got to hire an associate or two before I have a revolt on my hands."

"Why can't Aisha or Susan help with the search?" Leo asked.

"Because Aisha's interviewing potential daycare managers," Harri said as she snatched another chip and dipped it in La Churro's specialty, a creamy cilantro sauce. "Susan unfortunately is still defending Mother Defiant against Dewey and Cheatham's nuisance suit."

"You guys didn't get that thrown out?" Jeremy poured more mango margarita into her glass.

"Not before the rest of the partners filed for bankruptcy." Harri shook her head. "After Howard's arrest, Captain Mojave along with a bunch of their clients invoked their audit clauses. The forensic accountant they hired found a ton of issues." She shrugged. "On one hand, I feel bad for the bankruptcy trustee having to deal with that mess. On the other, Dewey and Cheatham's lawsuit against Mother Defiant is one of the few assets the firm has left."

"That's not fair." Leo scowled. "She was screwed over by those asshats, too. And she's punished for having the vagina to get out?"

"Yep." Harri dipped another chip in the cilantro cream sauce.

"How'd things go with my referral today?" From the way Jeremy trailed his straw through his drink, he knew something.

And she didn't need three guesses to figure out who he'd talked to.

"Did she tell you what she did to your referral?" Harri growled.

Jeremy exhaled. "Yes, she did. Is he okay?"

"Yeah," she admitted. "He was smart enough not to shoot through the outer wall and skid across the parking garage concrete. However, you weren't joking about the man having a chip on his shoulder."

"Sounds like Aisha does too these days." Jeremy shook his head.

"Because I'm generally the one who does something stupid?" She glared at him.

"I would never accuse you of being stupid." He selected a chip and dipped it in the bowl of red salsa. "Losing your temper on the other hand . . ." He shoved the chip in his mouth.

"Jaye, I told you we are all overworked right now." She leaned back against the padded seat. "I wasn't joking about the need to hire an associate or two before everyone quits on me." Her eyes burned. Despite her best efforts, her little firm was falling apart. And it seemed like everything she did made things worse.

"Honey, this isn't your fault." Leo reached across the table and took her hand in his. "Sudden success has its own type of pressure. In some ways, it's worse than failure."

Harri looked at Jeremy the same time as Leo.

Jeremy scowled at them. "You don't have to keep using me as an example."

"I didn't have to file for bankruptcy at twenty-one," Harri teased.

"And how many years did you refuse to date me after what your first assistant manager did to you?" Leo looked at his husband.

"Does this mean you're not taking my referral on as a client?" Jeremy asked, obviously changing the subject.

"I finished the intake interview, but—" Harri held up her hand when he opened his mouth. "The other partners need to review my notes, and they have a say. He already pissed off Aisha by blaming everyone else for his problems and for making the assumption she'd take his side because of the color of her skin."

"It sounds like maybe she was justified in her anger," Leo said. If anyone else know what it was like getting treated for his looks besides Aisha, it was Leo. It didn't help that his parents lived up to the Asian-American stereotype by trying to push him to go to Harvard medical school when his heart and soul was in art through hair design.

Deep down, Harri agreed Aisha had every reason to be pissed with Shadowstar, but she shouldn't have pushed the guy. She got damn lucky. With her superstrength, she could have killed him.

"I hate it when you guys point out my fights are my own fault," she grumbled.

"Fights, as in plural?" Jeremy frowned at her. "Who else have you been barking at besides me and Aisha?"

She could feel her cheeks heat up. "I may have pushed Tim too far this afternoon when I was complaining about Aisha wanting to go to Paris."

"Speaking of which—" Leo turned to Jeremy. "It's been a year. I'm still waiting on my honeymoon."

"You really want to do a foursome with Aisha and Rey in France?" Jeremy teased.

"Sweetie, if I had any chance of turning him to boys, I'd leave you in a heartbeat." Leo grinned.

"Good thing we both know that isn't going to happen," Jeremy shot back. "Besides, I could get him before you could."

"Boys!" Harri snapped. "We are not having this conversation about any of our brothers-in-law." She took a sip of margarita before she added, "And what's wrong with converting Tim?"

"Too much baggage," Jeremy and Leo said in unison.

"There's something else I need to ask you about," Jeremy added. "Has Betty said anything to you about a bridal shower?"

"Renata was adamant she didn't want one." Harri cocked her head. "It's a little late for her to change her mind. The place LaShun picked out isn't exactly a Betty-approved venue."

Jeremy rolled his eyes. "This isn't Renata talking. This is Betty. And it's probably our fault."

"Why the hell is it your fault?" Leo looked askance at his husband, then back at Harri.

"Because I didn't have a shower, and neither did you and Jaye." Harri pursed her lips. "Betty couldn't come to Aisha's first shower, and her wedding was a little rushed the second time around, so we didn't have a chance to plan anything."

"Ah." Leo nodded knowingly. "So she thinks Martin and Renata's wedding is her last chance."

"Unfortunately." Harri grimaced and looked at Jeremy. "How did you find out, and when is she planning on springing this on us?"

"Renata called Aisha who called me." He signaled their server and pointed to the empty pitcher before his attention returned to Harri. "Apparently, Betty refuses to listen to Renata and Aunt Queenie, and Betty plans to spring it on us when we get to Atlanta Friday night."

"Oh, god." Harri ran a hand over her face. Betty wasn't thinking straight. The Canyon Pointe contingent wouldn't get into Atlanta until eleven p.m. local time. There wouldn't be any chance to shop for presents if they had no warning. Or was that why she'd told Renata? Nope, Betty simply didn't think that deviously. At least, not on purpose. "She's in one of her obsessive moods. Well, you are her favorite daughter. If anyone can talk her down, it's you."

"I don't know if I can." Jeremy spread his fingers wide.

Harri groaned. The week in Atlanta would be crazy enough. And with all the bickering between her friends and family lately, the already-existing wedding stress would be the fuse to light the powder keg.

CHAPTER 11

<hr>

Aisha walked out of Mitch's room to find Tim pouring drinks in her kitchen. She eyed the bottle's label. "I'm pretty sure I didn't have single malt scotch in my cupboard."

"I ran across the hall and grabbed it from our place." He examined one of the glasses before he added an extra splash. "This conversation needs something stronger than wine, or even tequila."

That wasn't like Tim. Had Harri been even nastier to him this afternoon than Aisha realized?

"Well, if we're drinking your brand of rot gut, I need mine on the rocks," she said.

Tim turned, tugged the freezer drawer open, and scooped some ice into the second glass before he handed it to her.

She sat on a barstool again and pushed the bowl of cheddar crackers and nuts over to him. "Want some?"

He popped a few bits into his mouth and chewed slowly. She didn't need superpowers to realize he was incredibly uncomfortable, but it must be really bad if he didn't feel he could talk to Harri about what was bothering him. He washed down the snack food with half of the whiskey in his tumbler.

"You can't tell anyone about this." He exhaled wearily. "Not even Rey."

"Because he'll want to fix it for Harri?" Aisha cocked her head and regarded Tim. "Or because you want to fix it for her?"

"This isn't something any of us can fix for her." Tim tossed back the rest of his scotch. "And after the last couple of months, I thought she'd confide in you."

"But I threw a wrench in the works by planning to spend some time in Paris while my husband goes to school?" Aisha said sourly.

"Actually, I think the storage unit Grandma Harri left her is the real reason why she's been so cranky lately." Tim reached for the scotch bottle and refilled his glass.

"I take it you haven't had any luck tracking down the list of names you found in the boxes." Aisha popped a few more crackers in her mouth.

"No," Tim muttered. "Part of the problem is the adoption records from that far back aren't computerized. There's nothing in the Dewey and Cheatham network or the county courthouse database."

"Which means you would need to do a physical search," Aisha said. "Let me guess. Harri forbade you from breaking and entering?"

Tim swallowed the rest of his whiskey and set the tumbler down. "I know that's the right thing to do—"

"But you really want to break in and find that information for Harri." Aisha grinned.

"Please don't." Tim groaned. "I do not need another lecture."

"I wasn't going to lecture." Since she was no longer breastfeeding Mitch, she reached for the bottle of whiskey. With the changes to her physique, it took a lot more than a shot of single-malt scotch to get drunk these days. "There's a way to get you into Dewey and Cheatham legally. Susan's going to have to go to their offices for discovery in Mother Defiant's case. The trustee is refusing to spend money to make copies he doesn't have to."

"Isn't he required to preserve any and all assets of the debtor?"

"Very good, Mr. Canyon." Aisha smiled and saluted him with her tumbler before she took a sip. "If you go in with Susan and let's say you accidentally stumble on some records while you're looking for the men's room . . ."

Tim grinned. "And here, I thought Harri was the scary partner at your law firm."

"You'd better not call me a snake in the grass," she warned. The despised law school nickname had been one of the first things he said to her when they originally met.

"Don't feel like spending another couple of months in the hospital." He reached for the bottle and poured himself another shot.

"Think you could do it?" Aisha asked.

"I should be able to locate the adoption files." He swigged his scotch. "Searching through them and finding what we need will be the problem. That will take too long."

"Then you locate the files and give me a run down of the security system they have, and I'll take care of the rest."

"Don't you know Dewey and Cheatham's security system?" Tim frowned.

"I knew the code to turn the damn thing off and on." Aisha shrugged. "If I'd known I'd have to enter after hours post employment, I would have paid more attention."

Tim's frown deepened as he rubbed his chin. "How often did they change the system's passcode?"

Adrenaline rushed through her. "They never did in the fifteen years I worked there."

"The trustee should have," he said. "Know anything about him?"

She shook her head. "We could ask Susan."

"You know how she feels about my illegal shenanigans." Tim laughed.

"As good as she does about Arthur's." Aisha chuckled. "We tell her we are worried about her safety while she's in the Dewey and Cheatham offices. You're going to accompany her as a bodyguard."

"She's not that stupid," he pointed out.

"But she's not as stubborn as Harri. Plus she's still bothered by the jerks who trashed her parents' cabin last Christmas." Aisha sipped her drink. "She's not going to argue about you going with her after Howard tried to kill Harri."

"Damn, I wish we could reassure her. Arthur's been trying, but with cash and a burner phone, we'll probably never track down who hired those kids," Tim admitted. "I think it was a trial run by Howard and Delante to see how close their people could get to you, Susan, and Harri."

"You aren't the only one," Aisha grumbled.

Tim cleared his throat. "Do you mind if I change the subject?"

"Not at all." Relief seeped into her. She didn't like thinking about some of the events over the last year and a half. "What did you want to ask me?"

Tim dug in his pocket and set a small ring box on the counter. "I don't want to ruin Martin's wedding by asking her right now, but if I wait much longer, she will find it in our loft and freak out. Would you mind hanging onto it until she's ready?"

Despite her earlier argument with Harri, Aisha grinned. "It's about damn time, Canyon. Can I take a peek?"

He nodded.

She picked up the box and carefully opened it. Inside, a solitaire round-cut diamond set in a platinum band nestled in black velvet.

The loft door slid open. Rey entered with a bag that emitted the most delicious smells. He frowned as he eyed the ring. "Tim, aren't you supposed to be asking your girlfriend to marry you, not my wife?"

CHAPTER 12

—•◆•—

Harri's phone vibrated in her pocket. She pulled it out and read Tim's text.

"Traitor," she muttered and shoved the offending device back into her pocket.

"Who?" Leo asked as he scooped up the last bit of queso with his tortilla chip.

"Everyone who's pissed at me is having dinner together," she snarled.

"You need to stop bitching, girl. Timmy's the best thing to happen to you, and you know it," Jeremy warned.

"I know." She gulped the remainder of tequila and ice melt in her margarita glass. "Why can't I love someone like you and Aisha and LaShun and Martin? Tim's having dinner with Aisha and Rey instead of me. All because I asked him to stop running around like a fool."

Jeremy cocked his head. "Oh, honey, please tell me you didn't call him that."

She sniffed. "Why not? He wants to run around with the under-wear—"

"No man wants to be called a fool, baby doll." Leo shook his head. "If Jaye called me that, I'd definitely throw a fit, too."

"But—" Harri started.

"Harri, that man has done everything you've asked him to do, and then some." Jeremy frowned. "Are you going to keep changing the rules on him until he finally quits wanting to be with you like you did with Eddie? Because if you are, maybe you should let him go now."

"But I don't want him to leave," she wailed.

"Everything all right here?" Their waitress eyed Harri like she was a nuisance that needed to be ejected from the facility. Harri forced herself to focus on the server's nametag. Janna.

"Yes, ma'am," Harri said meekly. She couldn't collect on her year's worth of dinners from Jeremy if she got herself banned from La Churro's.

"Just some man trouble," Leo said. "You know how it is when one side's scared of commitment."

"Honey, if he ain't willing to put a ring on it, dump him." Janna scowled. "There's a lot of men out there."

"Janna, you definitely deserve a huge tip." Harri grinned at the waitress.

"Unfortunately, she's the one with the jitters." Jeremy pointed at Harri.

"I don't have jitters," she retorted.

"Then why won't you make it permanent?" Janna asked as she started clearing their appetizer plates.

"She made it clear if he even brings the subject up, she's out the door." Jeremy glared at her.

"Girl!" Leo looked at her askance.

"If you've changed you mind about getting hitched, you need to tell him," Janna said.

"That means admitting she was wrong before this," Jeremy said. "The only thing she hates worse than needing another human being is admitting she's wrong."

"I-I—" For some reason, Harri felt like she was falling into a trap. "I want him to ask me. He hasn't asked me." She stared at her empty glass. "I don't think he's ever going to ask me. I give him too much shit about his past."

"Is he cheating on you?" Janna asked.

"No," Harri admitted.

"If he's had a few girlfriends along the way, what's the big deal?" Janna said. "Surely, you've had a boyfriend or two." She grinned. "Now, if his exes are supervillains, then I can understand you being worried."

Harri looked up at their server through bleary eyes. "You sound like you're talking from experience."

"My ex didn't date a supervillain." Janna grimaced. "He just happened to be one of Miss Purrception's minions back in the day."

"Did she threaten you?" Leo asked.

Janna laughed. "Actually, she pulled me aside and told me I could do better."

"She told me I—" A sharp blow landed on Harri's shin. "Ow!" She glared at Jeremy. "What was that for?"

"Honey, you had an entire pitcher of margaritas by yourself and you're a private attorney these days." He scowled at her.

Janna chuckled. "I figured out who she was. The attorneys at Winters and Franklin have been all over the news for the last couple of years. Don't worry, Ms. Winters. I don't blab." She leaned a little closer. "Especially since y'all tip me well. I'd like to keep you as customers."

An idea blossomed in her brain, though it might be the tequila. "Would you like a job at our firm?"

Janna straightened. "I don't have a law degree, Ms. Winters."

"Actually, it would be to answer phones, but if you want to go back to school, that's definitely negotiable," Harri said.

"Ms. Winters, you've had a lot to drink—" Janna began.

"That's when she's the most honest." Jeremy laughed.

"I'm totally serious," Harri declared before she dug into her purse and pulled out a business card. "Would ten a.m. be a good time to come into our office tomorrow and meet the other partners?"

Janna took the card and examined it. "I'll need to think about it." She looked at Harri again and smiled. "But it doesn't hurt to talk. Your dinners should be ready. I'll be right back." She pivoted smoothly and headed for the kitchen with her hands full of dirty plates and bowls.

"I hope you're going to remember this in the morning," Jeremy teased.

"You are so lucky Leo is here," she shot back. "Else I'd bring up some of your past." She pulled her phone out and entered her meeting with Janna on her calendar.

Jeremy stuck his tongue out at her while Leo chuckled.

"Ms. Winters?"

Harri looked up from tucking her phone back in her purse. Travis Beckham stood by their booth, a tentative smile on his face. The former junior partner at Dewey and Cheatham was dressed in jeans and a polo shirt.

"Hi, Travis." She forced herself to smile at the man. After all the stories Aisha had told her about the lawyer and his shenanigans, he did save Harri's life when Howard Dewey wanted to shoot her. "How's things going with the trustee?"

"All the associates and junior partners were laid off this morning." Travis shuffled a little nervously. "Would you mind if I call you tomorrow and set up an appointment to talk with you?"

Harri cocked her head. "For representation?"

His expression turned sheepish. "No. I, um, accidentally overheard your conversation that you were looking for an associate."

"And?"

"I'd like to apply for the position."

CHAPTER 13

◆◆◆

"That's not funny, Rey." Aisha glared at her husband. "Tim was just showing me the ring, and he asked if he could leave it at our place for safekeeping."

"I told him two months ago the ring was safer on Harri's finger," Rey said as he crossed to the kitchen. He set his bags on the counter, leaned over them, and gave her a kiss.

"Didn't you text you were working the dinner shift for Rueben tonight?" she asked.

Rey shrugged. "The restaurant was slow, Emilio was there, and he needs the hours so Marta sent me home."

"He needs the hours?" Aisha cocked her head.

Rey folded his arms over his chest and scowled. "He won't accept help from me or his father for school."

It made a little sense. Emilio wanted to join in on Rey and Rueben's plans for a culinary empire, but he wanted, no, he needed to show he could pull his own weight. The Esperanza family's troubles had hit Emilio the hardest. Even his father Miguel admitted Emilio was the closest to Beatrice out of the four boys. Her death had devastated him.

"Not to mention, you're changing the subject," Rey continued before he faced Tim. "Why haven't you asked her yet?"

"Who? Harri or Aisha?" Tim teased.

"Dude, you had reserved a private room at Nolan's two months ago." Rey started pulling takeout containers from the bags. "Why didn't you follow through?"

"She discovered the contents of her grandmother's storage unit the night I planned to ask, and she refused to leave the apartment," Tim said sourly.

Rey grunted.

Aisha glared at her husband. "What was the bet with Arthur about, Rey?"

He grinned. "I figured Harri said no again. Arthur believed Tim chickened out. So I owe Arthur twenty bucks."

Tim scowled at Rey. "Harri was so wound up about the photos she found in the damn storage unit I couldn't do it. Then, it was too close to Martin and Renata's wedding, and I don't want to take away from their big day, but with Harri packing for Atlanta, no place in our loft is safe to hide anything from her."

A buzz came from Tim's pants. He pulled out his phone and checked the device. "And from the number of misspelled words in her text, she's already halfway through a pitcher of margaritas at La Churro's."

"You can have dinner with us and the spare bed if you need to stay here tonight," Rey offered before he looked at Aisha. "Jeremy and Leonardo are better equipped to deal with a drunk Harri."

She resisted the urge to sigh. As much as she wanted a quiet evening alone with her husband, his concern for the people around him was part of why she fell in love with him.

Aisha smiled and nodded. "We have plenty of food. I don't want to leave leftovers in the fridge when we head for Atlanta."

"I am also a little worried about Harri." Tim leaned his elbows on the bar. "God knows I don't have room to talk. I drowned my own grief in enough booze to fill Lake Del Oro, but she's been drinking a lot over the past month."

"Define a lot." Aisha pulled out plates from the cupboard.

"More than a couple of glasses of wine with dinner," Tim admitted.

Aisha exchanged a look with Rey, and her husband made a sour face.

"What's going on?" Tim asked.

"We know her bad mood isn't just about her grandmother's secret life," Aisha said.

Tim exhaled. "The Paris thing is bugging her, too." He shook his head. "If she didn't agree to couples counseling with Eddie, I doubt I can convince her to come with me."

"Eddie told you about that?" Aisha cocked her head. Harri's ex-husband was the stereotypical man's man. For him to seek counseling was tantamount to a declaration of love from the top of the Del Oro Bank Tower.

A wry smile crossed Tim's face. "You realize he did have my own secrets to hold over my head at the time if I blabbed. However, it is sad he felt he could only talk about his problems with a masked vigilante."

"Why wouldn't Harri go to couples counseling with Eddie?" Rey shared the contents of the take-home boxes among the three plates.

"Because it would have forced her to admit she didn't want the same things as Eddie." Aisha shook her head and turned to retrieve three clean glasses from the cupboard.

"That doesn't sound like her." Rey frowned.

"That's because she looks at you as a surrogate son, not a romantic partner, baby." Aisha scooped ice into the glasses.

"But that's exactly what I don't understand." Rey handed a full plate, silverware, and a napkin to Tim. "She has acted like a mother to me since we met. She dotes over both Grace and Mitch. Why does she keep denying she wants to be a parent?"

"Because it means she cares, baby," Aisha replied. "In her mind, she can walk away from the rest of us because we're adults and can take care of ourselves. Our kids have two parents, so in theory, she's not really responsible for them. But the idea of someone needing her, depending on her for everything, scares her to the bone. She's worried she'll be as bad a parent as her dad, or she'll die and leave them all alone like her mom."

"Oh." Rey handed a full plate to Aisha. "Now her anger about you going to Paris with me makes a lot more sense. She'd have the care and feeding of all the clients on her."

"Bingo." Aisha took her plate and walked around the island.

"But Susan will still be here." Rey pointed out as he reached for the refrigerator handle.

"If I could walk away to be with you in Paris, then Susan could, too, and Harri's back to being by herself." Aisha caught the bottle of water Rey tossed to her. "Which is why Tim hasn't asked her yet. She'll bolt faster than us at superspeed."

Rey nudged the fridge door shut, walked over to Tim, and handed their guest one of the two bottles he carried. "Violet Daze might help you out if we could get Harri to Vegas."

"Rey!" Aisha snapped. "You are not hypnotizing Harri into getting married!"

"Yeah," Tim said dryly. "I don't need a ménage à trois with Violet and Harri because that's what I'd have to do to keep Harri from killing me."

"A what?" Rey cocked his head.

"He mean a thruple," Aisha said.

"Oh." Rey sat down and dug into his dinner.

"Thanks for making me feel old," Tim grumbled. "Aren't you two supposed to be learning French anyway?"

Aisha's phone vibrated, thankfully interrupting Tim's whining. She pulled the device from her pocket and glanced at the caller ID before she thumbed the answer icon and reached for her scotch. "Hey, baby bro! What's shaking?"

"I really need your help." A tremor filtered through Martin's voice. "Renata wants to call off the wedding."

CHAPTER 14

"Oh." Harri wasn't sure this was the time or place for such a conversation, but on the other hand, she couldn't be rude to the man. She scooted over on the bench and patted the vinyl. "Have a seat."

Travis held up his hands. "I didn't mean to intrude on your dinner with your friends. This can wait until I make an appointment with you."

She turned to Jeremy and Leo, who were both staring at Travis with frank male appreciation. "Stop ogling the man, you two."

"Just because we're married—" Jeremy started.

"—doesn't mean we can't look," Leo finished.

Harri rolled her eyes and patted the vinyl upholstery again. "Have a seat, Travis. If you can survive these two, I'll have faith you can survive Winters and Franklin. And it's better if we get to know each other better without Aisha around."

Travis lowered himself to the bench. "I appreciate your time, Ms. Winters—"

"It's Harri," she said.

"Harri." He nodded. "And thank you again for speaking with the DA's office on my behalf."

"I knew Howard could be a shit." She pursed her lips and shook her head. "But you're the one who decided not to break the law by shooting me, which I do appreciate."

"It's one thing to use the gaps and loopholes in the legal codes." Travis stared at the colorful ceiling for a moment before he looked at Harri again. "It's another to ask me to commit felony murder." He sunk into the bench with a dejected expression. "God, I was so stupid."

"Wait a minute, Harri." Jeremy frowned at the younger attorney. "Is this the little schmuck who was promoted over Aisha?"

"Believe me, I wish I hadn't been," Travis muttered.

"His promotion may have been the trigger for her leaving Dewey and Cheatham," Harri said. "But she should have left those bozos long before then like Susan did."

Jeremy gestured with his half-full glass. "Ever since you took Captain Justice under your wing—"

"Don't you ever bring him up again." Harri glared at him. "I got the kid killed. I have to live with that every day."

"All I meant was you're killing yourself trying to be the social justice warrior Grandma Harri wanted you to be," Jeremy said softly.

"I'm not looking for a hand-out, Ms., ur, Harri." Travis straightened in his seat. "I admit Aisha Franklin is a better attorney than I am, but I can hold my own in negotiations and in court."

Janna walked around the corner her arms loaded with full plates. "Are you trying to recruit your entire staff here, Harri?"

She chuckled while Janna placed their dinners in front of them. "Not intentionally. This is Travis. He used to work with my partners, and he just got laid off, so put his order on my tab."

"No, you can't—" he protested.

"Hush, Travis." Janna waggled her index finger at him. "If Harri gets loud again, my manager will make me throw out her and you boys. Which means I lose my tip here. In which case, I will spit in your food. Now, where were you sitting?"

He waved toward his right. "I was seated in the section on the other side of the partition. The table with the rooster painting above it."

Janna smiled. "I'll let Rosita know so she doesn't think I'm poaching her tip. Be right back with your order." She grabbed their empty pitcher and strode toward the bar.

Travis turned to Harri with a concerned look. "What did she mean about you recruiting your staff here?"

Harri lowered her voice. "I'm trying to hire Janna as our new receptionist."

"Speaking of which, is Patty quitting?" Leo cut into his burrito.

"No, but she's not using her paralegal degree to its fullest, and—" Harri looked around and lowered her voice. "I'm not supposed to know this, but she's taking the LSAT next month. So if any of you blab—" She jabbed her knife in Travis's direction. "—and this includes you Beckham, I will shoot all of you with my taser."

"She's not joking, Travis," Jeremy said solemnly. "She nailed an assassin in his boys with her taser when she was in San Francisco earlier this year."

Harri grinned at Travis. "Consider your silence as your first test in seeking employment with Winters and Franklin."

"Yes, ma'am," he said gravely with a nod.

Before they left La Churro's, Harri made an appointment for Travis to come into the office tomorrow near the end of the day.

Jeremy insisted he and Leo drive her home. She didn't mind until he started his interrogation. That's when she knew climbing into the back seat of Jeremy's convertible was a bad idea.

"Are you deliberately trying to chase Aisha from the firm?"

"What? No!" she protested. "She's the one bitching about not having an associate but wants to take off to freaking Paris for a year."

"But Travis Beckham?" Jeremy shook his head. "You know how she feels about this weasel! She had to threaten to sic Rey on him and Stuart Cheatham to prevent them from doing a body cavity search while she was trying to walk out."

"I know," Harri bit out. "But she handled it just fine. Besides, he finally realizes how Howard Dewey was using him."

"He had to face life in prison before he stopped!"

"So I'm supposed to kick him to the curb? He's never going to find a job after Dewey and Cheatham because of their crappy reputation."

"What about everyone else who got laid off at Dewey and Cheatham today?" Jeremy yelled. "Are you going to hire them, too?"

"Maybe I will," Harri yelled back.

A growl vibrated low in Jeremy's throat. "Did you learn nothing from the Quantum Commander incident?"

"It's not like I'm making Travis a partner," Harri protested. "Besides I thought Aisha would enjoy ordering him around."

"That's not what you were really thinking, and we both know it," Jeremy snapped. "You're looking to get back at Aisha for wanting to be with her husband, and you know it."

"I am not!"

Leo peered over his shoulder at her. "Harri, sweetie, I didn't grow up with you like Jaye and Aisha did, but even I noticed you have some severe abandonment issues."

"This is about keeping the firm going!"

"Uh-huh." Jeremy's reflection grimaced. "Keep telling yourself that when it's all falling apart on you because you're acting like a selfish bitch."

"Calling me names is not fair!" Harri sniffed. The tequila was the reason her eyes were burning. Or maybe it was the exhaust from the truck in front of Jeremy's convertible. Dammit, she was not emotional because she didn't screw up.

A buzz came from the front seat. Jeremy pulled out his phone and handed it to Leo. "Would you check and see who it is, baby doll?"

"Oh, shit," Leo muttered.

"What?" Harri and Jeremy said at the same time.

"Aisha's calling an emergency family meeting," Leo said. "Renata wants to cancel the wedding."

CHAPTER 15

Aisha couldn't catch her breath. It felt like Ultramegaperson had punched her in her gut. This was bad. This was so much worse than Renata indicated earlier today.

The tumbler shattered in her grip. Ice, scotch, and glass shards sprayed across the counter.

"Shit," she muttered. "Not another one."

"Another what?" Martin said.

"I've got it." Tim snagged the roll of paper towels from its holder on the counter.

Rey held out his hand for the towels. "Let me."

"I can get it," Tim insisted.

"Maybe." Rey shot Tim a wry grin. "But the glass shards won't slice up my hands the way they will yours."

"Both of you, shut up!" Aisha floated up from her stool. The glass that hadn't penetrated her shirt tinkled across the hardwood below her. "I can't hear Martin."

"Are you okay?" her brother asked.

"I'm fine," she said. "Everybody's fine. I broke a glass. Give me a second." She put the call on mute. "Babe, you want to grab a clean shirt for me so I don't track glass and alcohol through the loft?"

Tim turned and faced the hallway Rey had darted down as she carefully peeled off her ruined t-shirt and dropped it in the puddle of scotch on the floor.

Rey came back with a purple t-shirt from a Nix charity event. Aisha slipped it on and yelled, "Clear!"

Rey held out his hand once again, and Tim conceded the point by silently handing over the roll of paper towels. Rey pulled the trash can closer to the counter before he started wiping up the mess Aisha had made.

She grabbed her phone from the counter, unmuted the microphone, and floated to the other side of the living room area. "Now, why is Renata calling off the wedding?"

"Between Mom throwing a last-minute bridal shower and Renee and Alexandro threatening to boycott if the new spouses come, she's at her wits end," Martin said. "She packed an overnight bag and left me a message saying she needed some time alone. Aisha, she's refusing to answer my calls and texts."

Across the room, Tim sat back down on his stool. He eyed the bottle of scotch for a moment, but he didn't reach for it. Good. She couldn't handle any more crises tonight.

"But she didn't say she was breaking up with you, right?" Aisha said.

Rey paused in scraping the glass and ice into the trash and glanced at her with a worried expression.

"No," Martin admitted.

"Okay, that's a plus." Aisha relaxed a fraction, and her toes touched the floor. She concentrated a bit more until her feet were fully in contact with the hardwood.

Rey tore off more towels, knelt, and mopped up the scotch on the floor, but it was obvious both he and Tim were not-so-subtly paying attention to her conversation.

"What do I do?" Martin asked. "I don't want to lose her."

Her heart ached for her baby brother. He was the romantic out of all the kids in their family, but this was something not even superpowers could fix. "Do you love her enough to call off the wedding if that's what she wants?"

"If that's what it takes, but I can't even tell her that if she won't answer her phone."

Rey stood and tossed the soaked towels in the trash can before he stalked across the room and held out his hand.

"Martin, Rey would like to talk to you," Aisha murmured.

"Okay." The dejection in her brother's voice made her own eyes well up.

"Martin, don't give up just yet," Rey said. "Can we call you back in five minutes?" There was a slight pause before Martin agreed. "Hang in there, *ese,*" Rey said before he ended the call and handed the phone back to Aisha.

"What's your plan?" she asked.

"We're gathering the sibling flock to work the problem." He smiled. "You text Jeremy and Harri. I'll call LaShun and Eric. You all can do a conference call on the firm phone downstairs."

He turned to Tim. "You are going to track down Renata." His bare foot made a sticky sound when he lifted it. "And I'm going to mop the floor while you two get this wedding back on track."

Rey lifted Tim and his stool and set them both down well away from the sticky spots on the floor.

"I really wish you wouldn't do shit like that," Tim grumbled.

"I think your ego can handle it this one time." Rey crossed to the utility closet, pulled out the mop, and inserted a pre-dampened cleaning cloth.

"You sure you'll be okay with Mitch?" Aisha asked while she walked to the door and slipped on her canvas sneakers.

"There's still some formula and applesauce in the fridge." Rey grinned at her. "If all else fails, I could feed him a vanilla milkshake."

"Rey," she growled. "You know about how I feel about giving him processed sugar."

"Just teasing, baby." He leaned over and kissed her forehead. "Go save your brother's wedding."

"Wait." Tim grabbed the ring box. "Where can I put this?"

Aisha and Rey exchanged a look before they turned back to Tim in unison and said, "Mitch's diaper caddy."

Tim charged down the hallway to Mitch's room. He was back before she finished her texts. She completed the messages to her foster siblings and best friends as she followed Tim to the elevator and hit send.

Unfortunately, saving Martin and Renata's wedding wasn't going to be as easy as saving a jumbo jet that had lost an engine.

CHAPTER 16

<hr>

Harri jumped as her own phone vibrated and buzzed in her pocket. She pulled out the device and checked it. "I got the SOS, too. What the heck happened after Renata called Aisha?"

"I don't know," Jeremy said. "I didn't have a chance to give Betty a call this afternoon. God only knows what she said or did to terrorize the poor girl."

"This can't be just about the stupid bridal shower," Harri said.

"Come on." Jeremy flipped on his turn signal to slide into the second lane and pass the truck. "You've known Betty as long as I have. She can be stubborn to her own detriment."

"She wouldn't deliberately sabotage one of her children's weddings," Harri argued.

"I'm not saying she did it deliberately." Jeremy glanced at her in his rearview mirror. "But she's got her own view of propriety, and you know as well as I do she wasn't happy about Aisha *having* to get married."

"Aisha didn't *have* to do anything," Harri snapped.

"That's not how Betty and Marvin saw it, honey," Jeremy said.

"You're shitting me?" Harri slumped in the back seat. Was she so wrapped up in her issues with Tim at the time she didn't notice how her foster parents were treating their own daughter?

"They never said anything in front of Aisha or Rey, nor would they,"

Jeremy said. "Aunt Queenie knocked some sense into them about the circumstances and how much Aisha wanted a baby. And don't you dare repeat any of this to Aisha or Rey."

"I won't." Harri chuckled. "Aunt Queenie is half in love with Rey herself. She'd whoop the crap out of me if I hurt him."

"Don't you mean 'in lust'?" Leo corrected.

"I'm just surprised Aunt Queenie didn't stop the bridal shower stupidity in its tracks," Harri said.

"We'll find out what happened soon enough." Jeremy whipped his convertible through the intersection onto Sixth Street. Thank heavens, there was very little traffic. Even Marta's parking lot was bare as they whizzed past the restaurant.

All three of them remained silent for the last three blocks. Jeremy hit the turn signal and pulled into the Lechuza Building's attached three-story garage. As soon as he pulled into a slot and threw the gear into park, Harri clambered over the side of the car.

"Harri!" Jeremy screamed. "I swear if you scratched my baby's paint—"

"Forget your damn car!" she hollered over her shoulder. "We've got a wedding to save!" She reached the door and slapped her palm on the biometric scanner. It was a good thing Tim installed these puppies because she drank enough mango margaritas she couldn't remember her social security number at the moment, much less a security code.

The lock beeped, and she shoved the door open. "Aisha!"

"We're in the conference room with coffee!" she shouted back.

Harri stopped in the middle of the reception area and stared at the ceiling. "I never realized how much sound echoes in here."

Jeremy and Leo each grabbed one of her arms and hauled her in the direction of the conference room.

"Hey!" she protested.

"You're the one yelling we needed to save the wedding," Jeremy grumbled under his breath.

They escorted her into the room. Aisha sat on the window side of the table, sipping her pixie barf from the intense peppermint odor. Tim sat on the south end of the table, staring intently at his laptop. A coffee carafe and a dish of creamers sat on the side closest to the door along with some mugs.

Jeremy grimaced and said, "I hope you have the full leaded version."

"Definitely. And I have LaShun, Eric, and Martin conferenced in." Aisha waved at the phone set in the middle of the table. "Harri, Jeremy, and Leo just arrived."

Harri dropped in a chair and reached for the carafe, but Jeremy slapped her fingers and grabbed the coffee. He poured and handed the mug to her. She reached for the vanilla creamer. It wasn't her first choice, but her stomach acid already churned between the alcohol and spicy food.

"Start from the beginning, Martin," Aisha said.

"Renata was stressed about Mom springing the bridal shower on her—"

"Wait! What bridal shower?" LaShun yelled.

Harri exchanged looks with both Jeremy and Aisha. For all Harri's teasing about Jeremy being the favorite, Betty and her eldest child were tighter than tight. If Betty hadn't run her crazy last-minute idea past LaShun, things were bad. Very, very bad.

While Martin ran through the tale Jeremy had already spun during dinner concerning their foster mother's sudden obsession with this bridal shower, Harri added a second creamer to her mug. She definitely needed to be sober for this conversation.

"Found her!" Tim shouted.

"Where?" Martin demanded.

"Slow down there, Marty baby" Jeremy said. "If Renata was upset enough to leave your condo, she needs a break from you, too."

"She called me earlier today, but . . ." Aisha got the look on her face when she was about to say something crazy.

Or something totally brilliant.

"Did you invite Lane to the wedding?" she asked.

"Yeah." Martin chuckled. "You know he spent Easter, the Fourth of July, and Aunt Queenie's birthday at Mom and Dad's."

Harri blinked. "Lane?"

"Mister Spectacular," Aisha said. "Martin, let me call him and ask him to check on her."

"You sure that's a good idea?" Martin said.

"I'll tell him we just want to make sure she's safe," Aisha reassured him.

"In the meantime, I'll call Mom about usurping my privileges as matron of honor," LaShun said.

"How about you and I do this together?" Jeremy eyed Harri. "Is it okay to use the company phone for that conference call?"

"Sure," she waved a hand. "You want Aisha and me to stay?"

"If you don't mind, let me and Jeremy handle it." For once, LaShun wasn't sounding superior. Actually, she sounded pretty worried. Another indication of major trouble in the Franklin clan.

"So, I'm just here for show?" Eric's voice rumbled through the speaker.

"No, honey, you're here to hold my hand and keep me from reaching through the phone lines to slap my mother silly for doing this to Renata," LaShun retorted.

"You want me to hold your hand, baby?" Leo looked Jeremy.

"No, go watch sportsball with Timmy and Rey." Jeremy gave his husband a quick peck on the lips.

Leo waited until they left the conference room and Aisha closed the door before he did a fist pump. "What's the score?"

"Copperheads up by two runs," Tim answered.

"Really?" Harri stared at her boyfriend. "We're in the middle of a crisis, and you two are worried about a baseball game?"

"The Copperheads are making a run for the pennant, Harri." Leo sounded like he was explaining it to a five-year-old. "They're the only team on the continent that's never won the championship, so yes, this is a big deal."

"Aisha, Renata is checked in at the Hyatt on Peachtree. Room 1215," Tim said before he and Leo charged for the elevator.

"You're not going with them." Aisha eyed Harri.

"No," she murmured. "You need to call Mister Spectacular, and then we need to talk."

Aisha merely nodded before heading into her office. Harri trudged behind her. She must still be angry about this morning's argument if she wasn't speaking.

Harri sat on the visitor chair and quietly sipped her coffee while Aisha dialed the number. Surprisingly, she put the call on the speaker.

"Hello?"

The smooth tenor sent a shiver down Harri's spine. If the man didn't already have a career as a super, he could make millions with voice-over work.

"Hi, Lane. It's Aisha Franklin and Harri Winters," Aisha said.

He chuckled. "That explains the 'Law Office of' on my caller ID."

"I know it's late in Atlanta, but I need a personal favor," she said. "My future sister-in-law had a major freak-out this evening—"

"Please tell me Renata and Martin didn't break up," Lane said. "It's the first time I actually have a date to a friend's wedding."

"It's not them," Aisha said. "Unfortunately, it's my mother."

"Oh, god. What did Betty do this time?"

Harri bit her lip to keep from laughing at Mister Spectacular's world-weary tone. He hadn't known the Franklins for a year yet, and even he could figure out who did something to tick off the rest of the family.

"It's not just Mom, though that's a huge part of it." Aisha leaned back in her chair. "Renata packed a bag and went to the downtown Hyatt. She's not answering anyone's calls and texts, so Martin's worried—"

"And you want an objective third party to check on her," Lane finished.

"If I'm out of line asking you for this, just say so."

"Nope, you're not out of line. Your family has been really gracious by including me in their family events." Scratching sounds came from the other end of the line. "Do you know her room number?"

Aisha rattled off the digits.

"I'll tell her I'm only doing a wellness check." He chuckled. "Do you need anything else?"

"No." Aisha sighed. "I really appreciate you doing this."

"How late is too late to call you back?" Lane asked. "I'll call your cell phone, but I don't want to wake the baby."

"Anytime is fine." Aisha laughed. "I don't think he's developed superhearing yet."

"I'll let you know what I find out," Lane said. The line clicked, and the buzz of a disconnected call filled the room.

Aisha leaned forward and pressed the button to close the connection. "You ready to apologize?"

"No, because I don't think I'm wrong." Harri took a deep breath and released. "But I also don't want to fight with you either."

"Yeah, we can call a truce until after the wedding." A wry expression filled Aisha's face.

"Um, hold that thought until you hear me out." Any positivity inside Harri about her idea died under her partner's withering gaze.

"All right." Aisha's nostrils flared. "I'm listening."

"I've got a potential associate coming in for an interview tomorrow afternoon."

"That's great! Why would I object to that?" Aisha gave her a confused look.

"It's Travis Beckham."

CHAPTER 17

Aisha stared at Harri. Surely, she hadn't heard what she thought she heard. "It's who?"

"Travis Beckham," Harri repeated.

Red flashed in Aisha's vision, and she could have sworn her blood boiled in her veins. Her butt slowly rose from her chair, but her fury didn't allow her to concentrate enough to regain control of her powers. "Out of the ten thousand attorneys in the Canyon Pointe metropolitan area and Lake County in general, you set up an interview with him!"

Harri held up her hands. "I know you have reasons to dislike him—"

"He sloughed off his work to the paralegals!" Aisha waved her hands wildly as she floated above her desk. "He sucked up to Howard Dewey to get promoted over me! And he was going to search my personal belongings after I quit!"

"First, there's no one here he can con into doing his job." Harri ticked her points off on her fingers. "Second, he's learned his lesson about Dewey, which is why Travis is not in jail and Howard is. Third, you can abuse him as much as you want. Fourth, he may have saved my life, but he's never going to be a partner here. And I'll make that damn clear tomorrow."

"You're damn right he'll never be a partner here! I will leave before I let that happen!" Aisha shouted.

"You're already planning to leave." The last word seemed to catch in Harri's throat.

Well, crap. Aisha focused until her sneakers touched the carpet. Was Harri that angry about the Garcia-Franklins heading to Paris for a year she'd throw Travis Beckham in Aisha's face? Or was she playing the guilt card?

"Why would you do this to me?" Aisha whispered.

"Because Travis did stop Howard from killing me, Cobblestone, and Judge Inunza." Harri sighed. "And because the trustee in the Dewey and Cheatham bankruptcy laid off all the associates and junior partners today. I think part of me wants to use Travis to give the trustee some shit since he won't drop the nuisance suit against Mother Defiant. I know you have some damn good reasons to dislike him, but I really think he wants a fresh start."

Aisha slowly lowered herself into her office chair. "You can't trust anyone from Dewey and Cheatham, Harri."

She lifted her chin. "I trust you and Susan."

Aisha didn't know what to say to that challenge. "If this turns into a Quantum Commander situation, I will be telling you 'I told you so' until the end of time."

"I know," Harri said solemnly.

"If Susan goes along with your insane plan, we sign him for a limited contract," Aisha bit out.

"I agree." Harri nodded.

Aisha tapped her fingernails on her desk. "If Susan says no, I'm siding with her."

"I wouldn't expect otherwise," Harri said.

"Why are you being so damn agreeable?" Aisha grumbled.

Harri sighed. "Honestly, I blame it on the mango margaritas."

"Mango?"

"Yeah, Mateo just added the flavor to the menu."

"It sounds good."

"It was. You wanna go after we get back from Atlanta?"

Aisha nodded. Damn, she hated it when she and Harri fought. They didn't always agree on things, but they usually could find a middle ground.

"One other thing—" Harri reached for her mug of coffee. "I think I may have a line on a new receptionist."

"Who?"

"Janna at La Churro's."

Aisha held her hand above her head. "Skinny, looks like she could play for the Scorpions, a few shades darker than me?"

"That's her."

Aisha shook her head and laughed. "Mateo's going to have a fit if you start poaching his staff."

"We give him more than enough money for alcohol alone to make it up to him," Harri shot back.

Aisha's cell phone buzzed, and both she and Harri jumped at the noise. The caller ID showed Renata's name and number.

Aisha tapped the answer icon. "Hey, Renata!"

"What the hell, Aisha!" Renata's language devolved into words in both English and Spanish Aisha prayed Mitch never learned. Renata finally took a breath before she blurted, "I can't believe you sent a super-hero to spy on me!"

"Is Lane there?" Aisha rubbed her forehead. Too bad her superpowers didn't do a damn thing for a stress-induced headache.

"Talk to her!" Renata screeched.

"Hey, Aisha," Lane said. It sounded like he was trying very hard not to laugh at her future sister-in-law. "Renata is fine. I don't know if she's more upset I saw the hot fudge sundae she was plowing through when I knocked on the door or I'm questioning her taste in movies since she had to pause *Romancing the Stone.*"

"Give me that phone!" Sounds of fumbling came through the receiver. "All I asked was for some alone time, and your damn brother couldn't even give me that." The last word ended with a sob.

"Oh, damn, sweetie." Aisha leaned her elbows on her desk. "This wasn't Martin. We were all worried about you. It's not like you to take off like this. I asked Lane just to make sure you're all right. I thought he'd be a neutral party."

"He-he—" Renata sniffled. "He caught me by surprise. Look, I know you mean well, and you probably haven't had a chance to talk to your mom today, but Betty called my mom, and now Mom's upset she didn't know about this shower. We had a huge screaming fight on the phone, so I turned the damn thing off. I just couldn't—I just—" Another sob followed the rush of words.

"I'm so sorry the parents are piling on you, sweetie," Aisha said.

"I thought if I paid for my own wedding, there wouldn't be much for them to fight about," Renata wailed. "But they're going out of their way to create things to argue over."

"Is Martin giving you the same shit everyone else is?" Aisha asked.

"No." Renata hiccupped. "I love him. A traditional wedding was the only thing he wanted, and the only thing I wanted was to make him happy."

"Sweetie, have you told Martin any of the things you just told me?" Aisha said.

"I wrote him a letter and tried to explain everything."

"Is this the note he found on the kitchen counter tonight when he got home?"

Renata gulped. "Yes."

"He didn't tell me what you wrote, but whatever it was, it scared him," Aisha said softly. "He thinks you're leaving him."

"I just needed some peace and quiet for one frigging night!" Renata started crying again.

"I get it, sweetie. Everyone's dumping on you, and you want to protect Martin." Aisha inhaled deeply and released the air. "Jeremy and LaShun are dealing with our mom as we speak. Can any of your brothers talk to your mom?"

Renata sniffed again. "Not really. Normally, I'd talk to Tyler about this kind of stuff, but he and Audrey ended up eloping because of our parents fighting. He's just going to tell me to go to Vegas like they did."

Can I at least tell Martin where you are?" Aisha said. "He really is worried about you."

"I don't know." Another sniff. "I feel like I'm failing him."

"Sweetie, he thinks he failed you." Aisha took a sip of her own coffee. She'd be up all night worrying even if it was decaf. At least it would give Rey a chance to sleep in if she were on baby duty.

"This isn't about Martin," Renata wailed. "But he wants the perfect wedding, and I can't deliver it!"

"You need to tell him that." Aisha set her cup on the warmer Tim had invented and turned it on. "I understand you need to spend the night in the hotel with ice cream and movies, but please, just call him and tell him what you told me."

"He's going to be pissed at me." Renata sobbed again.

"Maybe, but it'll be because you aren't telling him how you really feel, sweetie," Aisha said.

Lane murmured something in the background she couldn't catch even with her enhanced senses.

"I suppose you're right," Renata said. "I'm really sorry for yelling at you, Lane."

Masculine laughter rang in the background. "I expect a dance with the bride a week from Saturday."

"Lane just left. I'll call Martin, Aisha." Renata exhaled gustily. "I really do want to marry your brother, girl."

"Unfortunately, he comes with a ton of annoying relatives." Aisha laughed.

"No, a ton of relatives with a couple of annoying traits," Renata answered.

"Call me if you need to talk. I've had enough peppermint mocha I'll be up all night."

"Thanks. Sister."

Aisha thumbed the icon to end the call and rolled her head to ease the tension in her neck. "Now, where were we?"

"Setting up an interview with Janna," Harri prompted.

"Does that mean you don't want Veronica to sub—" Aisha glared at her buzzing cell phone. "Unknown number?"

"It's probably just Lane confirming Renata called Martin," Harri murmured.

Aisha resisted the urge to roll her eyes, but she had been the one to ask Lane for the favor.

She tapped the speaker icon to answer the call. "Hey, thanks for—"

"Franklin—need Owl—" The distorted male voice cried out in pain and the line went dead.

Chapter 18

Harri jerked upright in her seat and exchanged a worried look with Aisha. "Did you recognize the voice?"

Aisha shook her head.

"The number?"

Aisha shook her head again.

Harri pulled out her own phone and thumbed her boyfriend's speed dial icon. It rang once. Twice. A crowd cheering and male voices filled the speaker before Tim said, "More family drama?"

"No," she said. "Aisha just got a weird call on her smart phone from an unknown caller. I need you to trace the number."

"Guys, cool it. We have a real problem." The background noise from Tim's end went silent. "What did they say?"

"'Franklin. Need Owl.' Then there was a cry of pain before the line went dead," she said.

"Arthur, see if you can get a trace on Aisha's last incoming cell phone call," Tim said. "No, grab my laptop off the desk in the corner. Harri, were there any other noises you two recognized on that call?"

Harri glanced at Aisha who shook her head for a third time. "Nothing Aisha noticed beyond the heavy breathing."

Aisha's office door slammed open, making both women jump. Jeremy charged into the room, his face bright pick.

"I swear to every deity, past, present, and future, I'm going to kill Mama Betty!"

"We'll be upstairs in a few minutes, honey," Harri murmured before she ended the call to her boyfriend. "What happened?"

"She told both LaShun and me it's none of our damn business what she does." Jeremy blew out a deep breath. "When LaShun pointed out wedding etiquette dictates the bride's friends are responsible for throwing a shower, Betty said it's obvious none of us want to be friends with her future daughter-in-law, so it rested on her to welcome Renata into the family. Then she hung up on us."

Aisha's phone buzz, and she scanned the screen. "That's LaShun texting the same story." She chuckled. "With a few more colorful descriptions than you."

Harri looked up at Jeremy. "Did you and LaShun find out where this shower is supposed to be?"

He flopped in the chair next to her. "Some frickin' tea house in the Old Fourth Ward."

Harri leaned back in her own chair. "Has anyone RSVP'd to Betty?"

Aisha tapped out something on her phone. "LaShun said she got a couple of texts from a couple of friends of Renata's double-checking the time and place, but she didn't think anything about it."

"We're staying at the hotel where Martin and Renata are having their reception for a reason. We stick with our original plan, and then we'll put together the gift bags for the wedding guests Saturday evening."

"How do you plan to get the mothers to the surprise party LaShun planned?" Aisha said.

"I was just going to tell them we're having a family lunch with the bride." Harri grinned. "Maybe I should hire a couple of retired supervillains to kidnap them."

"That's not funny," Aisha snapped.

Harri sighed. "I'm sorry, girl. I'm not trying to start another fight with you, but this is Renata's wedding. Not mine. Not yours. And definitely not Betty's."

Aisha flashed a wry smile. "For once, we're in agreement. Jeremy?"

"You know I'm with you two." He grinned. "In fact, I doubt LaShun will pull her high-and-mighty act about how we all need to get along and act like a family. Betty really pissed her off. I can call the tea house and cancel Betty's reservation and explain to them what happened."

"And tell them to tell her she's the one who broke wedding etiquette," Harri said.

"Oh, I plan to go full queen on the manager of the tea house and make them return Betty's deposit." He shrugged. "But I'll cover it and the tip for the servers, so it's not a total loss for the staff."

"Then we stick to our plan, no matter how pissed the moms get." Harri pushed to her feet. "Even with a cup of coffee, I'm about to drop."

"What time is Beckham arriving for his interview?" Aisha asked. She didn't sound angry about the possibility of Travis working here, or even as hurt as she had a little bit ago.

"He's coming in at the end of the day to talk to me," Harri said. "I told him it would be a couple of weeks before I could bring him in for a full partners meeting."

"Let's check with Susan, but what about dinner with him at Marta's tomorrow night?" Aisha said as she and Jeremy stood, too.

"You want to do it that soon?" Harri said.

"It's better than stewing about him all this week and next when we've got a new family crisis crashing on our heads every couple of hours." Aisha shrugged.

"But we can't take him to Marta's," Harri protested. "You told me you introduced Rey to the Dewey and Cheatham staff as Captain Justice."

"So Rey stays in the kitchen while we have dinner." Aisha made a face. "If Travis works here, he's also going to see Steve. We can't avoid that. Or are you proposing to lock Steve in his office while Travis is in the building?"

"Why do you even want to bother having dinner with him?" Harri asked.

"So we can slap our own spyware on his phone." Aisha's grin was downright vicious. "Find out what he's really up to."

"She's got a point, Harri." Jeremy crossed his arms and smirked. "We've all been trailing behind the people who want us dead for over a year. It would be nice to be ahead of the game for once."

"You're both assuming Travis lied to me." Harri glared at them.

"Baby doll, I'd love to believe Mr. Beckham's little sob story." Jeremy shook his head. "But even I understand, you cannot put your clients at risk, much less all the kids who live in this building. If he stabs you in the back, you will never forgive yourself if your clients or the kids are hurt or killed."

"Damn," Aisha murmured. "I wish I'd come up with that argument."

"But what if Travis has been just as screwed over by the senior partners at Dewey and Cheatham as Aisha and Susan?" Harri asked.

"Then, we need to find out for sure," Aisha said. "Which takes us back to our own spyware."

"While you girls plot the destruction of a not-so-innocent man like a couple of supervillains, I'm going upstairs to gather my husband and go home." Jeremy marched toward the office door.

"Wait for us," Harri said.

"Speed it up, Shorty," he called over his shoulder.

"Aisha?" Harri turned back to her partner.

She laughed. "Go ahead. I'll lock up and meet you upstairs."

Sure enough, Aisha was waiting by the gate when the elevator groaned to a stop.

"Show off," Jeremy grumbled as he pulled back the car's gate.

"At least, she doesn't scatter my paperwork all over my office like her husband," Harri said.

"He did it again?" Aisha smacked her forehead. "I swear I talked to him about superspeeding through your office."

"I know you did." Harri made a face as they walked down the hallway to her door. "And no, he hasn't for over a month. Since you know what it's like to be a non-super, you're a little more conscientious of the side effects of using your powers."

Voices got louder as they approached her loft. She slid the door open. Tim, Rey and Steve were all on their phones in different corners of the living room. Arthur sat at the bar and scowled at Tim's laptop. For an instant, Harri worried their IT expert would resort to his supervillain persona to make the computer give up its secrets. Meanwhile, Leo cuddled on the couch with Mitch who was sucking down his evening snack.

One by one, Tim and the twins ended their calls.

"Well?" Harri prompted.

"All of the firm's clients are accounted for," he reported.

"And everyone is also checking with their non-firm acquaintances," Steve added.

"I've also called non-firm associates," Rey said. "So far, no one in the state is missing. The message tree is doing its thing. If anyone hears any news, they'll let us know."

Harri leaned on the counter. "Talk to me, Arthur."

He threw his hands in the air. "I've got nothing. Whoever called used the same trick we do for routing calls through dummy phone numbers. I lost the trace in Kyrgyzstan. I'm sorry, Harri."

"No reason to be sorry." She patted his shoulder. "I just wish the person had been able to say more."

"I can run it through voice recognition." Arthur looked up at her and shrugged. "But it's going to take time."

"What kind of time?" she asked.

"With everything I need to get done before we head to Atlanta?" He shook his head. "Even if I go down to the lab right now and get started, the analysis won't be done until we get back."

Harri eyed Aisha. "What do you think? If everyone we know answered roll call . . ."

"Our clients aren't the only ones who know my secret." She rubbed the back of her neck.

Harri muttered an obscenity.

Jeremy smacked the back of her head. "Language. Mitch doesn't need to know certain words until he's in kindergarten and beating up the playground bully."

She glared at him and rubbed the spot. "Did you guys call Eddie and Cal?"

"Yes," Tim said. "I also called Special Agent Nesmith."

"I checked in with Miguel and Dom," Steve said.

"And Emilio and Reuben are still at Marta's," Rey added. "I told them to call me when they get home."

"What's the score, Leo?" Harri asked.

"Bottom of the ninth," he reported. "Score's tied with runners on first and second, but the Copperheads have two outs. Esteban is up at bat. One strike and one ball."

The guys all groaned.

Even Harri and Aisha were drawn in by the next pitch on the TV screen. Esteban swung. With a loud crack, he launched the baseball into the air, dropped his bat and took off running.

Another round of moaning came from the guys as the opposing center fielder caught the pop-up fly. Even Mitch started wailing.

Jeremy looked at Harri. "Looks like I'll be enjoying your hospitality a little longer, Buttercup."

CHAPTER 19

The next morning, Aisha stared at her computer screen through blurry eyes. She couldn't even blame it on Tim's bottle of scotch. Staying up to watch the tenth through the fourteenth innings wasn't the smartest thing she'd ever done, but even she had been drawn in to the sports drama. The Copperheads finally managed to score the winning run at one-thirty-two.

Mitch woke up at five-fifty-nine.

She sipped more peppermint mocha and focused on the e-mail in front of her. The governor's office had sent a request, asking if Captain Justice's surviving family would object to a state holiday in his honor. Someone more objective than Harri or herself needed to make this call. She picked up the receiver and dialed Susan's extension.

"What's up, Aisha?" Susan was way too cheerful for nine-ten in the morning.

"You got a minute? I need an unbiased opinion on something."

"Sure," Susan chirped.

Aisha laid out the request from the governor's office.

"Feeling a little guilty about lying?" Susan asked.

"No." Aisha sighed and rubbed her eyes with her free hand. "The problem is I relive the grief of losing Rey every time the subject of Captain Justice comes up."

Susan hesitated a moment before she said, "I don't mean to get in your business, but have you talked to someone?"

"You sound like Jeremy and Tim," Aisha said.

"But not Harri?" Susan teased.

"When things went down last summer, she was going through her own grief." Aisha leaned back in her chair and stared at the plaster medallion on her office ceiling. "Besides assuming Rey was dead, we both blamed ourselves for what happened to Tim."

"Girl, as long as you and your husband are in the underwear game, you're going to be stuck with those feelings." Susan sighed. "You know the risks better than anyone. There's a shrink I send my clients to if you decide you want to deal with your issues in a more adult way than Harri."

"What's that supposed to mean?" Aisha snapped as she jerked upright.

"I mean I've noticed she's been going to La Churro's an awful lot over the last four months," Susan replied. "And there's the increasing number of bottles in the recycle bin every week. Honestly, I'm glad we're taking Beckham to Marta's tonight. Look, I'm not a tee-totaler by any stretch, but there has definitely been an uptick in her consumption."

Aisha tapped her fingers on her desk. Okay, so it wasn't her imagination. "Yeah, it started about the time she cleaned out Grandma Harri's storage unit."

"Did we spur the drinking along by telling her to lay off the other missing children?" Susan asked.

"It's the idea of Grandma Harri possibly funding Corvus and helping to take those children away from their parents that's really digging away under her skin," Aisha answered. Hell, she'd become just as guilty about increasing her intake of alcohol since she weaned Mitch last month. Maybe if she introduced it as she needed the help, Harri would respond better. "If I promise to talk to her about her drinking, will you give me a legal opinion on the request from the governor's office?"

"Technically, you can't stop the governor from signing an executive order or from introducing a more permanent bill in the legislature." Keys clicked in the background. "While it's good PR for the governor to ask nicely, it's going to be a little harder for you to complain now since Canyon Pointe already celebrates Captain Justice Day and you didn't protest the CJ Memorial in Mesa Rojo earlier this year." She was silent for a moment. "Aw, crap."

"What?"

"They didn't tell you who petitioned the governor's office for the holiday, did they?" Susan said.

"No," Aisha drawled. "Please tell me it wasn't the Super Rangers."

"It wasn't just the Super Rangers," Susan said. "It was nearly every kids' organization in the state. Cloverleafs, Youth Rodeo League, the Hispanic Junior Congress—"

"Okay, okay, I get it." Aisha squeezed her eyes shut. "The answer will say CJ's family is honored by the holiday and thank the governor for his dedication to CJ's memory—"

"But they will not attend due to privacy concerns, blah, blah, blah," Susan finished. "Just remind them that the estate has merchandising rights. There's a buttload of money for Mitch's education in promoting a Captain Justice holiday."

"Thanks for your ear." Aisha hung up the receiver, leaned her elbows on the desk, and rested her head on her forearms.

It may be the exhaustion talking, but every time a new Captain Justice request came across her desk, she wondered if this was the time their damn cover story blew up in their faces.

Five o'clock rolled around, and Aisha still had over half her to-do list to go. On the other hand, Harri had tried to find them an associate. As much as she disliked Travis Beckham, a little part of her wanted to get back at him for stealing the partnership from her at Dewey and Cheatham. Though in retrospect, losing the partnership at her previous employer had been the best thing that ever happened to her.

She shut down her computer, grabbed her purse and headed for the office door. Harri's door was closed. She glanced at Patty as she locked her door.

"Should I stay for a while?" their assistant asked.

Aisha shook her head as she approached Patty's desk. "Go home and hug Grace."

"Don't shove this one," Patty whispered fiercely as she stood. "He won't just phase through the stone and plaster like Shadowstar."

"I won't." Aisha held up the little finger of her right hand. "I pinky swear."

Susan rounded the corner from the back offices, her own bag slung over her shoulder. "We ready?"

"Let's go see." Aisha gestured her to follow before she said, "Have a good evening, Patty."

"You, too." She waved and disappeared behind the staircase. A few seconds later, the antique elevator wheezed to life.

Aisha crossed to Harri's office and knocked on the door.

"Come in!"

Aisha pushed the door open. Travis Beckham sat on the couch where Shadowstar had been yesterday. What was it about both men that drove her insane?

Oh, yeah. Their totally arrogant attitude.

She forced a smile. "You two ready to head out?"

"Yes." Harri rose and strode to her desk. "Who wants to drive?"

"It's only three blocks, girl," Susan teased.

"Says the woman who gets a sunburn when she opens her blinds," Aisha retorted. "I'll drive if you guys can deal with cracker crumbs coating every surface of my minivan."

"Works for me." Harri slung her bag over her head. "You tall people will have some leg room."

"You can always sit in Mitch's car seat." Aisha grinned.

Travis stood, looking at all of them like they were crazy. Good. If he was the one who decided to walk away, Aisha wouldn't be the bad guy.

The four of them walked through the atrium and out the side door to the garage. From the heat, Aisha knew her makeup wouldn't have survived the walk down to Marta's restaurant. Travis eyed Molly's motorcycle.

"Nice ride." He turned to the three ladies. "I'm guessing it's Susan's?"

They all laughed.

"No, it belongs to my son's babysitter." Aisha pulled her keys out of her jacket pocket and thumbed the fob button. The minivan's *beep* bounced around the concrete pillars.

"Oh, crap," Harri said as they approached the vehicle. "I wasn't thinking. Is she okay staying late tonight?"

"Yeah, it wasn't a problem." Aisha pressed the buttons to slide open the passenger door and raise the rear door. "She can watch her own shows here instead of the game shows her grandmother is hooked on."

"You live here?" Travis asked.

"We all do." Harri waved her hands at his dismayed expression. "It's not a requirement to work here."

Maybe Harri would drive him away after all.

"And no, we're not a commune," Aisha said. She reached into the back seat and unclipped Mitch's car seat. "It's a matter of convenience. We converted the top three floors into apartments."

Aisha walked around her minivan and set the baby seat in the cargo section while her three passengers climbed into the vehicle. She tapped the button to close the rear door.

Once she climbed onto the driver's seat, she turned the ignition switch. Blessed cold air blasted from the vents.

Sitting in the front passenger seat, Harri groaned. "That's better."

"Until we have to get out in two minutes," Aisha teased. She backed out of her parking space and headed toward the vehicle exit. As she checked traffic, she noticed a grayish-blue sedan parked across the street from the nail salon. The tint on the car's windows was much darker than the state's legal limit.

Some warning niggled in her brain. It felt like Corvus stalking them all over again. Damn, she didn't need more problems. Not when her family was threatening to implode over Martin and Renata's wedding. She debated saying something to Harri.

No, not with Travis in the minivan. It could wait unless the people in the grayish-blue sedan pulled some stupid stunt.

Her passengers stuck to small talk about the Copperheads chances of clinching a playoff berth while she drove the three blocks to Marta's. She kept an eye on her minivan's mirrors, but the sedan didn't follow them.

When they reached the restaurant, Harri noticed Aisha scanning the street. She raised a questioning eyebrow, and Aisha shook her head. Even though they'd been arguing the last few weeks over Aisha going to Paris with Rey, she knew when the chips were flying, Harri had her back.

At least, Aisha hoped Harri still did.

Inside the restaurant, Marta grabbed four menus and led them back to the booth the law firm staff affectionately referred to as Tim's Nest. It was the one seat where the people sitting on the rear bench could see every window and door in the establishment. Some of the older folks in the neighborhood were there for Marta's early bird specials, but otherwise, the restaurant wasn't too busy yet. Aisha and Harri made a point of taking the rear bench, which left Susan sitting next to their potential associate.

Once they were seated, Travis scanned the menu and whistled. "Not your typical Americanized Mexican food."

"Nope," Harri said. "And make sure you save room for dessert. Their chocolate cinnamon mousse is to die for."

He laid down the menu. "I have to admit this is a different way of interviewing than any other firm I've met with."

"Because . . ." Aisha prompted.

"When I was interviewing after law school, the interviewing partners would take me to Nolan's or Whitechapel for lunch." He grinned as he looked around. "I like this place much better."

"Let me guess," Susan said. "Those same partners won't give you the time of day now."

"I made my decision ten years ago," Travis answered. "I need to live with the consequences. However, my former employers have nothing to do with my skills as an attorney."

"I'll be blunt, Travis," Harri said. "It's going to take a lot to earn our trust, much less make partner at our firm."

He glanced across the table at Aisha. "I didn't expect otherwise."

She waited until Anna set down their glasses of water, the bowl of tortilla chips and two bowls each of tomato salsa and their creamy avocado dip and left before Aisha added, "And also, you're not going to be able to get anyone else to do your work. We simply don't have the manpower, which is why we're looking for a couple of associates."

Travis stared at her. "I'm assuming this has something to do with Lisa and Jeanette."

"Yes." Aisha reached for a chip.

"There's more to that story than you know." He shrugged. "Not that I expect you to believe me."

"Try us," Susan said as she dipped her chip in the bowl of salsa between her and Harri.

Travis took a sip of water first. "You know how big the senior partners were about billable hours. I got a lecture from Stuart that if I wanted to make partner, I needed to learn how to delegate. When I asked him what that meant, he said if I didn't make sure the ladies were eighty percent billable, they would be let go."

"So you did dump your work on them," Aisha commented.

"And I hustled to bring in new clients." Travis shook his head. "I quickly learned if they weren't white and fuckable, the senior partners would reject them." A bitter edge lay in his voice. He took another drink of water before he said, "What would be the policy if I brought a new client to Winters and Franklin?"

"It doesn't matter who brings in a client," Harri said. "I do the intake interview, and the partnership votes on each potential client. We will ask for the opinion of the rest of the staff, but the three of us do have the final say."

"The reason I ask—" Travis looked around before he lowered his voice. "There's quite a few clients who contacted me privately after I was let go yesterday. I simply don't have the resources to represent them properly."

"Give us one example," Aisha said.

"Captain Mojave."

Well, crap.

CHAPTER 20

Harri choked and managed turn her head before she spewed the mouthful of water across the table at the mention of the superhero's name.

"You okay there, Harri?" Susan asked.

Harri coughed some more into the crook of her elbow before she could breathe again. "Yeah, I'm fine. Just not the first super I expected." She eyed Travis. "Not bothering with the small fry, huh?"

He shrugged. "Mojave called me after I got home from dinner with you last night. I told him I was trying to get an interview with Winters and Franklin. He said if I got the job with you, he would definitely sign for representation. And yes, he terminated his representation with Dewey and Cheatham right after Howard's arrest."

"Just one little problem," Aisha said. "We can't sign him due to a conflict of interest."

Travis leaned back against the red vinyl. "Well, damn. I was hoping I could bring something to the table."

"It's been a while since I left Dewey and Cheatham, Aisha." Susan picked out another chip. "Are there any more clients we could have an ethics problem with?"

Aisha looked at the ceiling a moment, obviously running through a list in her mind. "Not that I know of unless it's someone they've picked up in the last year. Mojave is the big one."

"He's going to be disappointed," Travis murmured. "Can I ask what the conflict is?"

"You need to talk to him about it," Aisha said. "Though I'd be surprised if he admits it to you."

"Now, you've made me very curious." Travis raised his right eyebrow.

"We'll discuss it if we come to an agreement." Harri gave him a quick smile, but there more important things she needed to address with him. "There's something else you need to consider before you expect to join our firm. We have targets on our backs because our involvement with the downfall of Corvus."

"But they're all in prison except for General Trubble." Travis's attention flicked to each of the ladies. "Has he resurfaced?"

"Not that we know of." Harri glanced at Aisha. Did her strange phone call last night have something to do with the missing felon?

Harri turned back to Travis. "But with Howard Dewey's connections with Corvus, not only do you have to think about your family's safety, we have to consider our clients' and our families' safety if we decide to offer you a position with our firm."

"She's not joking either," Susan said in response to Travis's shocked expression. "Someone hired a couple of local thugs to trash my parents' house shortly after I became an associate."

"We've also been shot at, run off the road, chased by monsters—" Aisha ticked off the incidents on her fingers.

"Attempted strangulation, attempted bombing, attempted electrocution," Harri continued.

"And the people we've pissed off are now going after our clients," Susan finished. "Case in point, I can't use you in the lawsuit by Dewey and Cheatham against one of our clients."

"I told Howard suing Mother Defiant was a damn stupid idea," Travis muttered. "Unless Judge Cooper has totally lost his marbles, he's going to rule in favor of her."

"Except that's a huge chunk of change out of her pocket after he nickel and dimed her into ramen-ville," Aisha said sourly.

"Excuse me?" Travis blinked.

"Seriously, dude, that's why she left Dewey and Cheatham." Susan chuckled. "She got tired of living like a college student."

"That's impossible." He shook his head. "I negotiated her contract with Pan Learning Centers. She was pulling in mid-seven figures per year in that endorsement alone."

Harri exchanged looks with Aisha and Susan before she turned back to Travis. "Thanks for the tip."

Travis muttered an obscenity and stared out the window at the mural of Captain Justice on the side of the building next door for a long moment. When he turned back to Harri, he said, "I'll get you a list of all of Mother Defiant's licensing contracts. Even if you decide not to hire me, I want to do what I can to make things right with her."

⌒͜ ⌒

Harri was glad the rest of the dinner went smoothly. Aisha even lightened up a little towards Travis. Part of Harri wondered how her best friend would have regarded Susan if she hadn't also been a classmate of theirs at law school.

Best of all, Rey listened to his wife and stayed in the damn kitchen.

Once Travis drove off from the Lechuza Building's garage, Harri turned to go inside the side door. She wanted to make sure Tim and Arthur were able to plant their spyware on Travis's phone through hers or Aisha's devices. Susan followed, but Aisha stared up the street.

Harri walked back over to Aisha. "What's wrong?"

"See the gray-blue sedan near the danger sign on the fence?"

Susan joined them. "Yeah. It's the same make and model the NSB buys for their fleet."

"Except they purchase the tan version because the paint is cheaper," Aisha said. "And this one's windows are tinted darker than the state's legal limit."

"Think our NSB mole knows a certain special agent has been talking to us in more than his official capacity?" Harri asked.

"It's possible," Aisha admitted. "I'm going to walk down to the bodega. See if Celia or anyone else has noticed them."

"I'm coming with you," Susan said.

"Make it three," Harri said.

Aisha glared at Harri and Susan. "I can handle myself."

"You're not supposed to be going anywhere without a backup." Susan raised an eyebrow. "Or haven't you heard a dang thing that certain NSB special agent has repeatedly lectured you about?"

"And I want some chocolate chip cookie ice cream." Harri strode toward the sidewalk. Her partners followed. "How many people in the car?"

"Two," Aisha said.

There were a few pedestrians, but more cars using Sixth Street. Funny how people felt safer to be in this neighborhood with the Ghost Owl and Black Falcon patrolling the Canyon Block. Ironically, they weren't out quite as much these days, but just the idea of them protecting the north side of the city kept out a lot of the criminal element. Plus, the residents were proud of Rey, one of their own who did good, and he wanted to spread the wealth.

However, that didn't mean Harri and the other residents of the Lechuza Building didn't take precautions.

As they came even with the sedan across the street, Harri said, "I've got my taser. Susan?"

"Got my regular one and the miniature version."

"Miniature version?" Harri glanced at the red-head.

"You haven't noticed my new watch?" Susan wore a cat-that-ate-the-canary look as she held up her left wrist.

"I thought it was one of those phone watches or an exercise recorder." Harri examined the device and noticed the stylized TMC logo of Tim's company.

"It's the second prototype." Susan lowered her arm. "After Steelrose's attack, I asked Tim for something I could keep on my person instead of using my phone as a bomb in an emergency."

Harri grimaced. Susan and her passengers were damn lucky to be alive after the supervillain rolled Susan's rental car on the interstate. Susan's taser had flown out a broken window along with her purse.

"I think I need one of those for the next time someone tries to shoot me," Harri said.

"I don't know." Aisha grinned. "Tim and Steve said you did just fine with the full-sized version when you were in San Francisco."

"And yet people still keep trying to shoot me," Harri grumbled. "If you think about it, maybe that means I need a bigger version."

"I think court security will notice if you try to walk in with a taser the size of a grenade launcher," Susan teased.

They entered the bodega to find Celia waiting on Veronica and her daughter Josie.

"Just the ladies I need to talk to!" Harri strode up to the counter.

"You need some more painting done, Miz Harri?" Josie had a hopeful look on her face.

"Actually, I wanted to talk to your mom."

"Me?" Veronica's expression went from pleasant to irritated. "Did Josie do something?"

"No, no, no." Harri waved her hands. "Nothing like that. Aisha's baby brother is getting married next week. I was wondering if you would be willing to help Steve to cover the phones at our office."

Veronica laughed. "If you had asked me yesterday, I would have said yes in an instant, but I start a new job on Monday. Josie and I came here to get some ice cream to celebrate."

"That's wonderful!" Harri turned to Celia. "Her money is no good here. The celebratory sweets are on me." She leaned closer to Josie. "Go grab the large bag of Reese's Pieces. Those taste great with chocolate ice cream."

"Harri!" Veronica protested as the girl tore off for the candy section. "You're terrible."

"So where's the new job?"

Veronica grinned like a fool. "Saint Eugenia's in Hermanville."

"You and the kids are leaving Canyon Pointe?" Harri worked to keep the smile on her face, but her heart sank. Javier Esperanza, their building manager's teenage son, had a huge crush on Josie.

"Miguel and Julio are helping us drive what little belongings we have up to Hermanville this Saturday." Veronica's cheeks reddened. "Rey called some friends of his up there, and they found a nice place for us."

In other words, Rey paid the deposit and first month's rent. Harri would lay a month's income he'd asked Mother Defiant to pull some strings at both the private Catholic school she supported and for help to get Veronica and her children a place to live.

Josie raced back to the counter with her bag of candy.

"Good luck to you all." Harri hugged Veronica, then Josie.

"Good luck on what?" Susan said.

However, from Aisha's expression she'd either heard the conversation while she and Susan were retrieving ice cream from the freezer or Rey had already told her. Veronica did another round of explanations, which was followed by another round of hugs before Veronica and Josie left the store.

"It's nice of your brother to help Veronica move," Harri commented to Celia.

The bodega owner shrugged. "Everyone watches out for each other around here."

"I like that fact though." Harri stared at Veronica as she and Josie crossed the street. "I never thought I'd find a place to belong."

Celia smirked. "You know, I thought you were just another gringa looking to gentrify the Canyon Block when you moved here." She shook her head. "Rey was right. You are a good luck charm."

Harri snorted. "I'm sure Miguel will disagree after Frisco was kidnapped because of me."

"What? You think we didn't already have troubles?" Sarcasm oozed from Celia's tones. "No, you ladies are helping to rebuild this area."

"I'm only trying to do the right thing by Rey after he saved my life, so most of the credit goes to him, not me." Harri smiled. "He has a vision for this area that doesn't involve stepping on everyone. He wants to build something good. I can respect that."

"You keep talking about my husband like that, girl, and we're going to have a problem."

Harri looked over her shoulder at Aisha. "Shut your mouth. I like my men aged like a good scotch."

"Cut it out, you two." Susan shoved between Harri and Aisha and set the two pints of ice cream she carried on the counter. "We also wanted to ask if you noticed the blue sedan parked across the street."

"You mean the guys driving the same make and model as your NSB friends?" Celia grinned. "They've been parked out there off and on for the last few weeks. They started coming after the last time Agent Silver Fox visited Harri."

"Agent Silver Fox?" Harri cocked her head.

"That's what Monica at the nail salon calls him." Celia shook her head. "His partner goes in for a manicure every time he comes to talk to you. The four people rotating in the blue car are much younger. Three men and a woman. Ask Javier for pictures of them. His little crew of superhero sidekick wannabes have been keeping an eye on them."

"Crap," Harri muttered. "Here we go again."

"Thanks for the info, Celia." Aisha laid several large bills on the counter. "Keep the change."

"Tell the Owl to keep a close eye on these ones," Celia said as she bagged the ice cream, chips, and candy Susan and Aisha brought to the counter. "They may not be crows, but there are other birds just as deadly."

Sometimes, Harri wasn't sure whether to be afraid of Celia or be happy the bodega owner seemed to be on their side.

CHAPTER 21

Thursday night, Aisha couldn't stop the flurry of thoughts racing through her brain as she packed suitcases for her, Rey, and Mitch.

Thank goodness, both Martin and Renata had each texted to say they'd worked things out. In fact, she had invited him up to her hotel room Monday night after the initial meltdown. Renata said there was nothing like makeup sex in a hotel room, which was a little too much information. Martin merely said they had talked and Renata was more relaxed now.

As far as work issues went, Aisha was rather glad Harri suggested tabling the discussion of hiring associates until after they got back from Atlanta. Aisha still didn't trust Travis Beckham, but a couple of phone calls to former co-workers from Dewey and Cheatham confirmed some of what he said about the real reason he had dumped so much of his work on Lisa and Jeanette.

In the one small favor the universe granted, Janna decided she wanted-ed to cover phones in the mornings next week while Steve was in class. It would be a good test to see if she could handle the position of receptionist, or if she even liked it.

Besides, Miguel would be here to keep an eye on things. Age was starting to catch up to him in ways similar to Tim though Miguel had the excuse of construction for the wear and tear on his body, instead of supervillains and criminals. Without his older sons Dom or Emilio around, Miguel was able to hire some of his old crew to handle the jobs he couldn't. Maybe he need to set up a proper business front in one of the second floor offices.

The elevator whined to life, and the voices of Rey and Emilio drifted up the shaft. Once Rey finished his cooking degree, it would be Emilio's turn to head to Paris.

Aisha had drafted the forms for Rey's proposed corporation for the guys' restaurants and the holding company for the real estate. She had been a little surprised how many investors her husband already had lined up. Most of them were superheroes. But when she asked Susan to look over the documents, her partner said it would be a conflict of interest. Susan had already talked to Rey about leasing a small retail space for her jewelry, art, and crafts store.

Everyone was moving on with their lives. Everyone except Harri.

She walked over to Rey's dresser and started pulling out clothes. It was going to be dang hot in Atlanta even this late in the year. She selected four pairs of his nicer shorts and matching polos and t-shirts. When she reached for socks, her fingers brushed against the ring box he'd tucked in that drawer for Tim. Rey hadn't felt comfortable after he accidentally stuffed it in Mitch's diaper bag and carried the ring to the park.

Aisha pulled out the velvet-covered box and opened it. Harri was so determined to keep her walls up, even though Tim had given up nearly everything he had left to be what she said she wanted. What if that wasn't enough? Would Harri ever let herself just be happy?

"I'm starting to get a complex the way you stare at that ring." Rey crossed the bedroom and pulled Aisha into his arms. He smelled of grilled beef, onions, and cilantro.

She hugged him back. "You've got nothing to worry about, baby."

She looked into his gold eyes. "Ever." She broke their embrace and snapped the box shut. "It's Harri that worries me."

"You two have another fight?" he asked.

"No, we called a truce until after the wedding." She brushed past him to return the box to its hiding place and pulled out several pairs of everyday socks.

"Something's wrong though," he stated as he pulled his work t-shirt over his head and placed it in the hamper.

"Too many things running through my head tonight." She tossed his socks in his suitcase before she perched on the mattress to watch him strip. It was one of the few pleasures she had these days. "Mainly, I'm a little worried Harri's going to break Tim's heart."

Rey paused in unbuttoning his jeans. "What did she say? Is she kicking him out?"

"No, she hasn't said anything like that." Aisha pursed her lips. "I'm finally realizing just how stuck in the past she is. I'm worried that when Tim finally does ask her to marry him, she'll reject him because of all the crap she's gone through."

Rey nostrils flared as he kicked off his shoes. "You can't fix her, Aisha. Any more than you can fix me."

Something in his attitude reminded her of Susan's suggestion earlier in the week. "Have you been seeing Susan's therapist?"

His eyes narrowed. "Would you think less of me if I have?"

"Hell, no!" At his warning look, she lowered her voice. The last thing they needed was to wake up Mitch. Not with the crazy travel day tomorrow. "Definitely not. It's just Harri's usually Little Miss Fix-it. How did Susan talk you into going?"

"She didn't. I asked for the referral." Rey sat next to Aisha on the bed and took her hand in his. "My anger, my fury, about what happened to me last year was eating me alive. Intellectually, I know none of it was Steve's fault, but he's here. Professor Paranoia isn't. I needed help finding ways to deal, and I couldn't lay it all on you. That isn't fair either."

She threaded her fingers between his and squeezed gently. "I just wished you had told me. I understand why though, and this won't leave our bedroom."

"Back to our original subject, Harri's got to want to let Tim into her heart." Rey lifted Aisha's hand and kissed the back. "If it's any consolation, I worry she's going to throw away what she has, too. With both you and Tim."

She sighed and leaned her head against his shoulder. "Things with the firm are going so well. I really thought it would be safe to work from Paris."

"Are you having second thoughts?" Rey murmured.

"About us going to Paris? No." Aisha sighed again. "About becoming business partners with Harri? Yes." She chuckled. "The odd part is I was never worried about money coming between us."

Rey's laughter rumbled through his chest. "I never though I'd have money." He kissed her hair. "Let me get a shower. We can talk more about this when we're alone in our hotel room. Tomorrow is going to be a very long day."

⌦

Aisha smiled at the organized chaos in the garage Friday afternoon. Harri's buddy Dopinder had recruited three other cabs in addition to his own to drive the Lechuza Building group to the airport.

Unfortunately, their driver Sanjay wore the exclusive commemorative Captain Justice t-shirt she'd licensed last year, and it poked at the scars on her heart. Once they were on the road, he admitted Dopinder had given it to him as a bribe for today's trip.

"We all thought Dopinder was driving for an escort service," Sanjay said excitedly. "He was being so secretive and doing pickups and drop-offs at such odd hours. Prepaid superhero fares are so much better!"

"You really can't be repeating this information, Sanjay," Aisha said. "It could put all of you in potential danger."

"Not to mention, my wife only works for superheroes," Rey said from the front seat.

Sanjay waved his right hand in a dismissive gesture. "Dopinder's my cousin, and he already threatened to dump my body in the middle of Del Oro if I breathed a word of this to anyone. But can I ask you one question, Ms. Franklin?"

"I'll answer if I can," she said cautiously.

The cab driver turned serious. "Was Captain Justice really as nice as everyone says he was?"

Rey shot her a surreptitious glance from the front seat.

"He was better," she said wistfully. "He really cared about the people and doing the right thing."

"I only met him once," Sanjay said softly. "My son really wanted to see him. He looked my son in the eye and took time to talk to him. He did that with all the children. I wanted—" He cleared his throat. "I guess I wanted to know that it wasn't an act."

"No." Aisha's eyes stung, and she blinked. "No, Captain Justice definitely wasn't putting on an act."

"I know you can't tell me for sure." Sanjay sniffed. "But I pray his children know what a great man their father was."

Aisha didn't know what to say to that.

"Do you have any other children, Sanjay?" Rey asked.

"Our second one is due any day now," their driver replied in a happy tone. "A girl this time."

"Congratulations!" Rey grinned at Sanjay. They began trading stories of their own childhoods and what they hoped for their children.

Aisha smiled to herself. She had no doubt Sanjay's baby would be receiving a gift basket from the Ghost Owl and Black Falcon when they returned from Atlanta. She just wished the fear of losing Rey again didn't haunt her every time the subject of Captain Justice came up.

Chapter 22

As her found family flew through the night sky onboard the massive jet, Harri snuggled Grace on her lap while her goddaughter sucked on an orange lollipop. Both Patty and Arthur protested over the sweet until one of the men sitting behind them got ugly over Grace's crying. It wasn't the toddler's fault the only other way to equalize the air pressure in her ears was by wailing like a banshee.

Déjà vu hit Harri hard. Except it was her sitting in Grandma Harri's lap while they were on a much smaller plane. Mom had chided Grandma Harri about giving Harri a cherry sucker, and Grandma Harri snapped, "Would you prefer torturing the child with the pain in her ears?"

Harri cocked her head to glance between the seats, The Franklin-Garcias sat in the row before Harri and Tim. Mitch snuggled in his baby seat, Rey snored softly, and Aisha read on her phone.

"Everything okay?" Tim whispered.

"Yeah." Harri smiled at him. "I think our godson has his parents' tolerance for high altitudes."

"As opposed to our goddaughter?" He grinned.

"I wonder if she was picking up Arthur's discomfort as well as experiencing her own," Harri murmured. Aisha had discovered Arthur's sensitivity to the changes in air pressure when they flew to Memphis last winter to meet with a company who wanted to license his paint removal formula.

"It wouldn't surprise me," Tim admitted. "Grace is a very perceptive young lady."

"That she is."

And Grace felt nice cuddled against Harri's chest.

Not that she'd ever admit that fact to anyone.

Atlanta's airport was as busy and as hot and as humid as usual when they arrived even though it was after ten p.m. local time. Harri split her team into three groups: one to take care of the needs of the children, one to pick up their luggage and a third to pick up their rental vehicles.

"Why do I have to pick up luggage with the guys?" Susan whined.

"Because I received a nasty phone call, a nasty e-mail, and a nasty snail mail letter from the CEO of a certain rental company to the effect that if I ever let you rent a car on the firm account again, they will terminate our business relationship," Harri said.

"Neither of those incidents were my fault, and they were covered by the insurance I bought," Susan protested.

"If this were an emergency, I would argue your case." Harri glared at her partner. "However, this. Is. Not. An. Emergency."

"Let it go, baby doll," Jeremy said. "This is not a battle you'll win today."

Susan huffed off with Tim, Rey, and Leo.

Harri rolled her eyes and led Jeremy and Arthur towards the rental counters.

"I could have helped with the luggage," Arthur said softly.

"Yeah, you could have," Harri admitted. The last thing she wanted was to step on Arthur's budding ego. "But you also haven't wrecked two vehicles in the space of a day like both of my law partners have."

"Aisha only wrecked her BMW because Corvus was chasing her and Rey," Arthur said with a confused look.

"She's not talking about that day." Jeremy laughed.

"Aunt Queenie was teaching Aisha how to drive," Harri said. "In Aunt Queenie's ancient Buick that had more metal than most battleships built today. Aisha managed to hit her dad's car. When she backed up, she didn't check behind her. Smacked right into a cop car. There wasn't even a scratch to Aunt Queenie's land yacht."

"Oh, dear." Arthur looked horrified. "How much trouble did she get in?"

"That summer she was waitressing at Nolan's." Jeremy grinned and shook his head. "Aunt Queenie paid for the damages to the other two cars, but every penny Aisha earned went to pay Aunt Queenie back."

"But the cop—" Arthur frowned.

"He was a sergeant who lived on the same block." Harri grinned at Arthur. "Luckily, he was fairly cool about the whole thing. He was only pissed about having to file the extra paperwork."

The three of them reached the counter for the rental agency. Luckily, it wasn't as busy as the rest of the airport. They had the keys for the rental vehicles in short order, and they headed out to the pickup area.

The air outside Atlanta International felt like Harri breathed boiling water. As the clerk at the counter said, all three vehicles were parked together.

"You couldn't get anything more flashy than minivans, girlfriend," Jeremy complained. "And in a color other than tan or gray."

"I'm sorry they don't appeal to your esthetic sensibilities, Jaye," she shot back. "Next time, make your own damn reservations." She pressed the button of the fob she'd been assigned. The light grey van in the middle beeped and flashed its lights.

"I think the colors are appropriate," Arthur said. "The scheme does match a certain firm client."

"Suck up," Jeremy muttered.

"Let's get the rest of the crew," Harri said to forestall any more bickering. They were all exhausted from the six-hour flight. Not to mention the two-hour time difference meant they'd have to eat dinner in the hotel's bar.

She'd forgotten how big Atlanta's airport was. They had to drive nearly all the way around the thing to get into the correct lanes for passenger pickup. It took long enough Tim called her twice to make sure everything was okay.

She pulled into the temporary parking lane. Leo, Rey, Susan, and Tim charged through the automatic doors with rental carts packed full of luggage and baby paraphernalia. Aisha and Patty followed with their children in their arms and diaper bags slung over their shoulders.

"You want me to drive to the hotel?" Aisha murmured while Harri strapped the infant carrier base in the rear passenger seat.

"No," Harri grumbled. "I have a freakin' GPS, and I have driven in Atlanta traffic before." She pinched her finger, and several nasty words tried to make themselves known before she settled on, "Dang it!" She shook her hand.

"You just seem a little tense," Aisha commented.

Harri gritted her teeth. Why was Aisha treating her like she was freaking helpless? She jammed the latch plate into the buckle. This time, the parts locked like they should. The last thing she needed was to be fighting with Aisha in the middle of Martin's big week.

She stepped out of the way so Aisha could snap Mitch's infant carrier in place and lowered her voice though Rey would still hear her. "I'm second-guessing leaving Steve and the Esperanzas alone in the building if we have more trouble brewing."

Aisha straightened. Mitch was out cold again despite the jostling.

"Qiang and Connor will be over a couple of nights a week to have dinner with Steve," she said. "Plus, Cobblestone and Nix will keep an eye on the place."

"You told them about our new watchers already, didn't you?" Harri accused.

"Just like you didn't tell Tim about the watchers so he'd come to Atlanta," Aisha whispered.

"What are you two conspiring to do?" Tim said behind Harri.

She jumped and whirled around to face him. "I swear I'm putting a bell on you when we get home."

"And any time I see two girls whispering, a load of trouble follows." Tim crossed his arms.

"Girls?" Harri's blood simmered under her skin.

"Yeah, girls." He scowled at her and then Aisha. "So what is it you didn't want me to know so I would come to Atlanta?"

His joints may be going to hell, but he sure hadn't lost his hearing considering how noisy the pickup area was. Aisha climbed into the back seat with her son to avoid the potential battle.

"I'll tell you on the way to the hotel." Harri stepped backwards. "Rey! You riding with us?"

"I'm going with Arthur and Patty," he called back.

Of course, he was. Mom and Dad were fighting as the rest of the staff would say. She'd pulled the same chickenshit maneuver when she was a kid. However, Rey wasn't—

Actually, he was young enough to be hers and Tim's son. She kept forgetting that because he was married to her best friend.

Harri hit the fob button to close the minivan's sliding door before she glared at Tim. "Don't even suggest that you drive."

He held up his hands. "Wasn't going to."

While she rounded the vehicle, he climbed into the front passenger seat. Once she was belted in and started the engine, she said, "There's been a blue sedan parked on our block for the last few days."

"That's what you two were whispering about?" Tim started laughing.

"What's going on?" Harri snapped.

"I cut a deal with Special Agent Nesmith." Tim's chuckles died down but didn't disappear. "He recruited four NSB agents he trusted to protect Steve and the Esperanzas while we are gone in exchange for developing more secure comm units for the bureau."

Harri clenched her fingers around the steering wheel. "And you didn't mention this because . . ."

"I didn't want to worry you." He glanced over his shoulder at Aisha. "Any of you. With the increase in your workloads, you were all stressed out, and you needed this next week to focus on your duties as bridesmaids."

"You still should have told me," Harri growled.

"Like you told me?" he pointed out.

As much as she wanted to clobber her boyfriend, he was trying to do the right thing. "If you ever hide anything from me again, I'll shoot you with my taser in the same place I shot that assassin in San Francisco."

Aisha snorted behind Harri, but Tim wore a totally serious mien. "Yes, ma'am."

Harri checked her mirrors before she pulled away from the curb. Part of her hoped he was right that this next week, she would only have to worry about wedding things. The rest of her knew she wouldn't get that lucky.

CHAPTER 23

The incessant ringing of Aisha's cell phone intruded on whatever dream she'd been enjoying. Half-afraid it was a superhero alert she'd missed, she jerked upright and checked the caller ID.

Nope. It was a different kind of emergency. Mom. Best to get this over with.

Aisha thumbed the answer icon as she lay back on the mattress and pillow. "Hey, Mom."

"How dare you ditch the bridal shower I'm throwing today!" she screeched.

Dang. Aisha would have laid her next endorsement check LaShun told Mom neither the bride nor the bridesmaids were going to the tea house. Jeremy had asked the manager not to tell Mom that her refund had been issued until Monday.

"Mom, it's six on the morning for me, I have very sensitive hearing, and I never received any invitation to any bridal shower." Aisha looked at the rest of the bed and the travel crib. She listened, but no one moved in the living area of the suite either. Rey must have taken Mitch down to one of the hotel restaurants for breakfast to let her sleep.

"Don't you sass me, young lady!" Mom screeched again.

"If you don't want to be sassed, why are you breaking wedding etiquette?" Aisha pinched the bridge of her nose. Her phone beeped quietly. She lifted it to see the display. LaShun. No doubt her sister was trying to warn her, so she let it go to voicemail.

"Because Renata's so-called friends and bridesmaids can't follow wedding etiquette!"

The decibel level got to be too much for Aisha's poor ears. She laid her phone on her stomach.

"Mom, Renata has more on her plate besides the wedding," Aisha said patiently. "Though she scheduled the ceremony for the second quarter of her company's fiscal year, which is her quietest time at work, the board of directors moved up the IPO ironically because she's doing a fantastic job.

"And because Renata is so overloaded, she asked us not to have a formal shower. Her friends and bridesmaids acceded to her wishes because this is *her* day. Not yours, not mine, not anyone else's. And I know damn well, both Aunt Queenie and Renata have explained this to you more than once."

The second line beeped again with a call from LaShun. Aisha ignored it. She could only deal with one insane family member at a time.

"This has nothing to do with me," Mom snapped. "Her mother was going to have the shower in some sleazy place downtown."

Well, that was news. Had Renee told Renata she planned a shower? Or did she not have the chance to before Mom co-opted the party?

"Do you mean Renee was going to have the party at her nightclub?" Despite Aisha's efforts, this whole conversation gnawed on her one last thread of patience.

"That establishment is no place for a young couple to start their new life together," Mom spat.

The thread snapped with that comment. "So, letting the groom's mother try to break up the couple is?"

Mom hesitated. "Wh-what are you talking about?"

"Renata walked out on Martin Monday night, Mom, because all of the pressure you're putting on her to have this damn shower."

"That's not my fault!"

Nope, it never was. Aisha pinched the bridge of her nose again.

"Mom, stop and think a minute. You didn't even tell LaShun about this shower, and you tell her everything. Don't you think that deep down you knew you were crossing a line if you didn't want to tell LaShun?"

"I didn't want her to think she had to help me with the arrangements," Mom protested.

"That's BS, Mom, and we both know it."

"I don't need your backtalk, Aisha Claudette Franklin!" The line abruptly died.

She thumbed the icon to end the call. Only for her phone to start ringing immediately. LaShun for the third time. Aisha tapped the answer icon.

Before she could say a word, LaShun said, "Whatever you do, don't answer any calls from Mom!"

"Too late."

LaShun cursed. In the background, Aisha could hear her nephew Devon say, "Mom, language! Not in front of Mitch!"

"Sorry, girl." LaShun sighed. "I tried. Why don't you grab Harri and Tim and join the rest of us for breakfast at the buffet?"

Pounding echoed through the hotel suite. With her damn superhearing, Aisha winced at the noise and Harri screaming her name.

"We'll be down in a few minutes. Mom just called Harri."

LaShun groaned. "This is getting ridiculous."

"Tell me about it." Aisha climbed out of the bed, trudged out to the suite's main door, and yanked it open. Thank goodness, she learned her lesson about sleeping at a hotel years ago, so she had on shorts and a t-shirt.

A red-faced Harri had paused to take a breath. An equally red-faced Tim mouthed above her head, "I'm sorry. I tried to stop her."

"Good morning, Harri." Aisha held up her phone. "Say hi to LaShun. Let me change and we'll meet the rest downstairs for breakfast.

As soon as Aisha, Harri, and Tim reached the buffet, LaShun raced across the dining room, grabbed Aisha in a bear hug, and whispered, "Dad and Aunt Queenie are here."

Aisha snickered. "So they made a run for it."

LaShun released her and nodded. She turned to Harri and Tim, but their hugs didn't have the desperate quality that Aisha's hug had.

They followed LaShun to the four tables shoved together at the back of the dining area. It wasn't just Dad and Aunt Queenie at the table with the Canyon Pointe and Portland contingents of the family. Renata and Martin were there, too.

Aisha circled the table, greeting everyone. It didn't surprise her one bit that Devon was sitting on Rey's left. Thankfully, her husband took her nephew's literal hero worship in stride. However, Jada barely acknowledged Aisha's hug and kiss. The girl was thoroughly glued to her phone's screen.

Aisha took the free seat next to Aunt Queenie. Her great-aunt leaned closer and asked, "Where's that studly brother-in-law of yours?"

"Back home covering the phones, and I told you before he's taken."

Aunt Queenie sniffed. "Is he still lollygagging over that girl who won't give him the time of day?"

"She's giving him time now." Aisha chuckled. "And I know dang well you gave him the advice on how to get her attention."

"Pish." Aunt Queenie waved her hand in a dismissive gesture. "I only gave him the benefit of my years of wisdom."

"And extensive experience with the opposite sex." Harri set her plate at an empty chair across from Aisha.

"It's not just the opposite sex," Aunt Queenie said with a mischievous smile. Her statement even drew Jada's attention from her phone.

Aisha laughed. "You need to save those comments for when Mom's around."

"These comments are why I miss you." Harri came around to give the elderly woman a hug.

"It's good to see you, Ma Petite." Aunt Queenie patted Harri's back. She eyed Tim who gave her a friendly smile. "However, I do question your taste in men."

Tim's smile turned chilly. "Excuse me?"

"Oh, get the broomstick out of your ass, Canyon," Aunt Queenie chided. "I know damn well my girls proved your innocence." She looked up at Harri. "If you were going to chase a ginger, you should have pursued Prince Harry before he got hitched."

Aisha laughed. "That's all I need in my life. Harri-squared."

At least, Tim relaxed at Aunt Queenie's teasing. He sat in the empty chair between Jada's and Harri's. "So, I take it you and Marvin are hiding from Betty, too."

"Not just them," Jada said solemnly. "Grandma has gone bat crap crazy over Uncle Martin's wedding."

"We're not hiding. We're escaping from a crazy woman," Aunt Queenie retorted. "Betty could give some of those supervillains a run for their money." She reached under the table and squeezed Aisha's hand. "This is why I never married. Too much fussing from the people who aren't even jumping the broom. They think they have a say in the new family because the folks are part of their old family. Some people just can't let go. Like Betty."

Some people just can't let go. The words echoed inside Aisha's head and wrapped themselves around the picture of Lydia Baxter-Murray and her son Pablo on the wall of Harri's guest bedroom back in Canyon Pointe. What if it was neither her father Eagle Forever nor then Lt. Byron S. Trubble who Lydia wanted to escape from?

CHAPTER 24

After breakfast, Harri leaned her elbows on her knees and listened as poor Renata vented. The other three bridesmaids, Patty, and Susan remained quiet on the couches and chairs in Harri and Tim's suite.

Thank goodness, the guys took the kids down to the hotel's Olympic-sized swimming pool while the women and Jeremy dealt with the stressed out bride.

When Renata finished and dabbed at her eyes with a tissue, LaShun made a slashing motion with the blade of her hand. "I'm sorry both of our mothers are acting like bitches, but this is your wedding. We will all support you with whatever you want to do."

Jeremy and all the other women nodded and made supporting comments.

"I'm just so freakin' tired." Renata leaned against the back of the chair. "If I wasn't losing so much money on the deposits and the IPO wasn't Monday, I'd hogtie Martin and throw him on a plane for Las Vegas."

"I don't mean to stir the pot, but do you think moving up the IPO is someone's way of trying to get you out of the way at your company by hoping it fails?" Patty asked.

"Oh, I know it is." Renata grimaced. "One of the board members Fletcher Haynes wanted his son named as CEO, but the rest of the board voted him down. It was his idea to move up the IPO based on my excellent financials."

"Do you need help from us on that front?" Harri asked. "A forensic accountant to see if Haynes is doing something shady?"

"If he is, it's with his own money." Renata shook her head. "I think he's just hoping I break from the stress, so he can complain that women can't handle the burden of running a company. But at the office, my people are doing the jobs I tell them to do. Mom and Betty though—" She threw her hands in the air. "They don't listen to a thing I say."

"I can take care of this right now for you," Harri said. "Do you want them to join us at lunch this afternoon?"

"I—" Renata's shoulders sagged. "I do if they can behave themselves."

"Honey, if I can taser an assassin in the nuts, I can handle two crazy mothers." Harri grinned. "Text me your mom's number." She thumbed through her contacts and tapped Betty's number.

"So have my daughters come to their senses?" Betty snapped.

"Hello to you, too, Betty, and yes, we have." Harri rose and paced on the carpet between the living area and the kitchenette. "A van will pick you up in front of your house at twelve-thirty this afternoon."

"And if I don't come?" But there was a hint of trepidation in Betty's voice.

"Do you really want my supers to drag you kicking and screaming out of your house?"

"Aisha wouldn't do such a thing," Betty retorted.

"Who said she was the only one with me?" Harri said sweetly. "Twelve-thirty." She disconnected the call.

Renata and Lashun stared at Susan and Patty, who played up the bluff by high-fiving each other. On the other hand, Aisha and Jeremy were trying very hard not to laugh.

Harri tapped the number Renata had texted her.

After two rings, a professional-sounding woman crisply said, "Renee Estevez."

"Ms. Estevez, this Harri Winters of the Law Offices of Winters and Franklin," Harri said equally crisply. "A van will pick you up in front of your house at twelve-thirty this afternoon."

"Excuse me?" Renee said with a haughty tone. "You presume to order me around?"

"No, I don't presume," Harri said coolly. "I am giving you a direct order. If you don't obey, then you're telling your daughter how you really feel about her. So cut the crap about both the bridal shower and your ex-husband, and take the chance to make up with your only daughter. Twelve-thirty, Renee." She clicked to end the call and turned off the sound and vibrations notices.

She looked at the group sitting around the living area. "I'm surprised they haven't called the rest of you."

"Baby doll, we were smart enough to turn off our phones sound and vibrators," Jeremy said smugly.

"You know how to turn off a vibrator?" LaShun mocked. "There's a first for everything."

Even Jeremy joined in the laughter at LaShun's teasing.

At twelve-twenty-nine, Harri pulled in front of the Franklins' historic Victorian. Betty sat on the porch swing and stared at the minivan.

"What's she doing?" Renata murmured from behind the driver's seat.

"Proving a point," LaShun answered.

When the time of the dashboard display flipped to twelve-thirty,

Betty stood and stalked down the porch steps and walkway to the curb. She opened the front passenger door, climbed into the minivan, and buckled herself in the seat all without saying a word.

Harri smiled to herself as she pulled back into what passed for traffic in this neighborhood. Marvin's grandfather had built this house at the turn of the twentieth century. It represented the closest to a real family in her life since Harri's mother died three decades ago.

She knew damn well Betty would explode when they arrived at their destination. And part of her couldn't wait until then to throw Betty's secretiveness back in her face.

CHAPTER 25

The party, because Aisha couldn't really call it a bridal shower, was in full swing. She grinned and held up her mimosa to LaShun. "Marvelous job, matron of honor."

"Baby sister, I can organize with the best of them." LaShun clinked her glass against Aisha's. "I think it's time to pay the piper."

Mom stalked toward them, a scowl on her face. "Why didn't you two tell me about this?"

"This what?" LaShun tried for an innocent air.

"This is a bridal shower," Mom hissed.

"No, it's not." LaShun lifted her chin.

"I lost my deposit." Mom glared at LaShun.

"No, you didn't," Aisha said. "Jeremy got it back for you. They'll have the refund check ready Monday morning."

"I don't understand why you kept the shower a secret from me," Mom protested.

"Renata did not want a shower." LaShun enunciated each syllable with the precision of a hammer. "You didn't listen to her, and you hurt her feelings."

"I-I—" Mom looked flabbergasted at the turnabout.

"We took her feelings into account, and we proposed a lunch or drinks with her." Aisha grinned. "She didn't specify which or when, so LaShun organized this little get-together."

"Aisha, Jeremy, and Harri paid for it," LaShun added. "It was supposed to be a surprise. We didn't tell you because we know neither you nor Renee could keep quiet."

"And then, our own mother tries to steal the matron of honor's thunder without a by-you-leave," Aisha added. "I wonder what the etiquette books would say about that." She took a sip of her mimosa and watched Mom's reaction.

She cleared her throat. "I-I guess I owe you girls and Jeremy apologies."

Behind her, Harri approached and obviously heard the last part of what Mom said. "You think, Betty?"

Mom winced at the sarcasm dripping from those three words. "And I apologize for yelling at you on the phone this morning, Harri."

"What I want is an apology for ruining the first quality time I've had with my boyfriend in the last four weeks," Harri growled.

Mom's hands fluttered, like they always did when anyone brought up sex. "Harriet Mathilda Winters! That's an inappropriate subject to discuss in public!"

"Then you'd better apologize for yelling at me first thing in the morning," Aisha said smoothly. "Because if Harri asks me to hang you from the Bank of America Plaza antenna, I will."

"I didn't call you until eight," Mom grumbled.

"My circadian rhythm said it was six a.m." Aisha raised an eyebrow. It was the same expression Mom used when Aisha hemmed and hawed after getting caught doing something she knew dang well she wasn't supposed to do.

"And you couldn't wait until six-thirty before you chewed me out," Harri grumbled.

Jeremy approached them. "Ooo! Are we giving the mother of the groom a difficult time for her nasty phone calls this morning?"

"I didn't talk to you this morning!" Betty protested.

"But, you did call me at six-fifteen this morning," Jeremy said with a smug expression. "I was smart enough to turn off my phone last night, and you were smart enough not to leave a message I could use against you right now."

Betty's mouth opened and closed like a beached fish desperate for oxygen. Finally, her shoulders slumped. "You're all right. I screwed up, and I apologize to all four of you for my . . . atrocious behavior."

"There's one more person you need to apologize to, Mom." Aisha gestured at the bride, sitting across the room with a handful of her college friends.

"I'll wait until she'd not so busy," Mom murmured.

"Nuh-uh, that is not how our family works." LaShun waggled her index finger at Mom. "Now, you march your fanny over to that girl, and you apologize."

Aisha had to stifle a laugh. Her sister's statement was a word-for-word lecture Mom had delivered to LaShun after an incident with one of the neighbor girls.

Recognizing she was on the losing end of the argument, Mom grumbled, "Fine."

The four of them watched her approach Renata and apologize. Their soon-to-be sister-in-law stood and enveloped Mom in a tight hug.

"Y'all know we're going to be up late putting together those wedding guest gift bags," Jeremy said.

"Are you joking?" LaShun whispered. "We've got a bridesmaid with superspeed."

"I am not doing all those bags by myself," Aisha hissed.

"Not to mention, superspeed can cause its own problems," Harri added. "Do you really want the friction to accidentally set the hotel on fire?"

"Point taken." LaShun sighed. "The old-fashioned way it is."

Aisha knew her sisters were teasing, but she had a disturbing suspicion she'd need her superpowers for Martin and Renata's big day before her baby brother could say his vows.

Chapter 26

<hr>

Monday morning, Harri wanted to take a hot poker and stab someone with it. Preferably the hotel's event manager at the other end of the phone.

"What do you mean the Estevez-Franklin wedding reception was canceled?" Harri bit out. "The bride and groom finalized the menu four weeks ago."

"I'm sorry, ma'am, but we got a call from Ms. Estevez on Friday cancelling their reception," the event manager said. "I even confirmed with her that she would lose her deposit, and she said she understood."

"Friday as in three days ago?" Harri glanced at Aisha sitting on the chair at the suite's desk. She frowned back as she listened to the conversation with her damn superhearing.

"Even though the first wedding guests checked in that night in the block of rooms she asked for when she scheduled her reception here?" Harri growled.

The event manager sighed. "Frankly, Ms. Winters, it's not unusual for a reception to be cancelled at the last minute and guests not being notified in time. I assure you that your and your party will still receive the rate Ms. Estevez originally negotiated."

"Gimme." Jeremy waggled his fingers.

She handed over her phone.

"This is Jeremy Harkness, Ms. Estevez's wedding planner," he barked into the device.

"You're not listed on the contract," the manager huffed.

"That's because I just took over," Jeremy growled. "You do realize Ms. Estevez is the CEO of Guidestar Healthcare?"

"Uh-huh," the event manager stammered.

"Like most female CEO's, she thought she could do everything," Jeremy snapped. "She should have hired me last year, but now, I'm discovering it's you who is totally incompetent!"

"Now, just a minute—"

"I have Ms. Estevez's planning notebook," Jeremy said. "She only called the florist on Friday to confirm the church where the flowers should be delivered. The florist got a second call less than five minutes later by someone claiming to be Ms. Estevez and wanting to cancel the order. How did you verify it was Ms. Estevez you spoke to on Friday?"

Holy crap! Harri exchanged looks with Aisha and LaShun. They appeared as baffled as she was.

"I-I-I—" The event manager couldn't make a coherent word, much less a sentence.

"Look, you and I both know you've already got the food for the reception," Jeremy said soothingly. "And you don't have another event already scheduled for the Poseidon Room. Tell the banquet staff the reception is back on, and you're going to pay them double. My client will cover half the cost because the staff has been inconvenienced, and you're going to pay the other half for not calling my client directly to confirm any cancellation."

Harri blinked. Why the hell was Jeremy wasting his time with his artsy, fartsy crap? He could negotiate better than half the attorneys she'd met in her career.

"Th-that sounds acceptable, Mr. Harkness," the event manager blurted out. "Please tell Ms. Estevez I'm very sorry about the mix-up."

"You do your job, and she never has to know," Jeremy purred.

"Thank you, Mr. Harkness." The event manager's gulp was audible from across the room. "May I have a number where I can reach you?"

Jeremy rattled off his own number. Once he was satisfied, he thumbed the end call icon and handed the phone back to Harri.

"What the hell was that?" she asked.

He waved at Renata's planner she had been using for her wedding. "I had the florist, remember? She told me that some asshat called her to cancel that order, but when she asked the caller to confirm the flowers, the caller knew the colors, but not the actual varieties, so the florist knew something was up."

"In other words, we've got to call every vendor to make sure we're not going to have a hitch on Saturday," Harri said.

"Renata's got her dress, the programs, and the birdseed roses for their exit according to Aunt Queenie," LaShun said.

"Good grief, that leaves nearly everyone else." Aisha looked aghast. "Give me the salon."

"I'll take the bakery and the church." LaShun took the business cards from Jeremy's outstretched hand. "I'm glad both families attend the same place of worship."

He looked at Harri. "If you take the wedding organist and the quartet for the reception, I'll handle the photographer and the bar service."

She took the cards he gave her and started dialing. When the guys got back from the Center for Civil and Human Rights, she'd have Arthur do some snooping for her. Someone was deliberately trying to sabotage Renata's wedding, and they damn well weren't going to get away with it.

CHAPTER 27

━━◆●◆━━

Aisha breathed a little sigh of relief. She'd actually met the salon manager Gloria at Saturday's luncheon. The lady was a high school friend of Renata's and knew immediately the woman calling her on Friday was not her long-time buddy and client. Gloria hadn't brought up the weird call because she hadn't wanted to upset Renata.

"Do you know anyone who might have a grievance against Renata?"

Gloria was silent for a moment. "If we were still in high school, I'd say it was Amber Henderson. Renata beat her out for homecoming queen our senior year, and it didn't sit well with Amber or her mama. But I don't think Amber even lives in Atlanta anymore."

"Any one else might want to mess with Renata?" Aisha asked.

"I don't personally know many of the folks she hangs out with these days other than your brother," Gloria said. "And Renata's not the type to complain about someone if they were giving her a hard time. I'm sorry, darling. I guess I'm not much help."

"Actually, I'm glad Renata has friends like you, Gloria," Aisha said. "Thank you for your assistance." She ended the call.

"The church is okay," LaShun said. "Luckily, Pastor Jackson answered the phone Friday. He knew damn well it wasn't Renata. He contacted Mrs. Green, the organist, before the joker called her."

Jeremy cracked up as he got off his call. "The baker doing the wedding cake is an old friend of Renee's. When she got the call from our fake Renata, she immediately switched to Spanish. Our fake got very upset and hung up."

Harri walked back into the living room. "Apparently, the string quartet wasn't contacted by our mystery lady." She flopped on the couch across from LaShun and Aisha. "They've only been in contact with Martin."

"Come on, Harri. That makes total sense. You know how picky Martin is about music." LaShun chuckled.

"What about the bar service?" Aisha asked.

"Once again, Renata's personal relationships save the day." Jeremy dropped next to Harri on the other couch. "She used to work for the owner on the weekends she wasn't at her mom's nightclub while she was in college. He knew it wasn't Renata thanks to caller ID."

"So our culprit isn't the brightest crayon in the box, but she's petty as hell." Aisha tapped her right index finger against her lips. "We can have Tim and Arthur do some digging."

"Already planned on it as soon as they get back from sightseeing," Harri said. "I just wonder if it's not someone at Guidestar—"

Aisha's phone rang. She checked the caller ID. Crap. Lane wouldn't be calling unless it was important.

"What's—"

"Turn on ENN right now, Aisha." Lane wasn't this upset when gunmen took him and his fans hostage last year at his annual Christmas event.

"ENN," she repeated to Harri, who leaned over sideways to grab the remote from the end table.

"This is bad, Aisha," Lane said. "This is so bad. I'm already getting calls from news outlets. I keep telling them to call my lawyers. Aisha, my girlfriend is going to kill me when she sees this!"

The big screen TV winked to life. It took Harri a couple of precious seconds to find the right channel in the hotel's system. Finally, the screen filled with the faces of former actress Kat Jennings and quasi-journalist Stone Rickman. But behind them was the PR horror currently freaking out Lane.

It was a blurry, but recognizable, shot of Lane at Renata's hotel room door and her in her bathrobe.

Chapter 28

"Oh, fuck." Harri could only stare with her mouth hanging open as the disaster played out onscreen.

Kat Jennings smiled brightly at the camera as she read the teleprompter. "For those of you just joining us, today's top story is the alleged affair between Atlanta's favorite superhero Lane Chisholm, otherwise known as Mister Spectacular, and Renata Estevez, who broke gender and race barriers last year when she was named the CEO of Guidestar Healthcare, one of Atlanta's top employers."

"While Mister Spectacular is one of the few capes out of the closet, he's never been photographed in public with a companion of any gender," Stone said. "Given how he lives his life as an open superhero, what would attract him to a high-powered CEO like Estevez?"

"I think you hit the nail," Kat replied. "They are both powerful, but in different ways. However, does this mean Renata Estevez's wedding this weekend to up-and-coming music producer Martin Franklin is over? They met during their college years when both worked at Club 1999, which is owned by Renee Estevez, Renata's mother. However, according to sources, they didn't start dating until three years ago."

"This news comes the same day Guidestar Healthcare made its first public offering—"

The vibration in her shorts pocket made Harri jump. She yanked out her phone. Its tiny screen displayed the office's main number. She thumbed the control as she stood and headed for the bedroom. "Winters."

"Harri, there's a ton of reporters outside banging on the glass." A thread of panic filled Janna's voice though she was desperately trying to maintain her composure. "I don't know what to do."

Aisha followed Harri into the bedroom and closed the door. She must have ended the call with Lane.

"Janna, Aisha is here. I'm going to put you on speaker." Harri thumbed the control.

Their temporary receptionist's voice blasted out of the tiny device. "I did exactly as you guys instructed. I've said no comment to everyone who's called about Mister Spectacular, but these people are loud and scary."

"Janna, the reporters are nothing like supervillains," Aisha said. "They can't break that glass. Cobblestone and Nix are supposed to be watching the place. Have you called them?"

"Nix was supposed to be here this morning, but her phone kept rolling over to voicemail. Mr. Cobblestone answered his phone, and he's on his way here."

"He'll keep his word, Janna," Harri said. "When you hang up with us, text Steve and warn him we've got barbarians at the gates—"

Janna's earsplitting shriek would have deafened Harri if she had been holding the phone near her head. Even Aisha winced.

"Don't scare me like that!" Janna lectured. "Sorry, Nix just popped out of the basement door."

A woman's voice said something in the background before Nix chirped, "Hey, ladies! How's Hotlanta?"

"It could be a lot better," Harri grumbled. "What's the situation there?"

"I saw the crowd, and it took me a little while to backtrack through the subway tunnels." The superhero chuckled. "Outside, we've all the local affiliates and the cable news networks, the *Tribune*, and the Hot 99.6 van just parked across the street." Nix laughed. "We officially have enough of a crowd to report them to the cops for being a nuisance."

"Janna, can you do that?" Harri asked.

"Throwing out assholes, I can handle." Their temporary receptionist didn't sound on the verge of panic like she had a minute ago.

"Call the CPPD and report them for blocking the entrance to our business."

"Gotcha, Harri! Good luck!" Janna ended the call.

Only for Aisha's phone to start ringing. She looked at the caller ID. "Damn, it's Nella." She grimaced as she answered the call on speaker. "No comment."

"Dang, girl!" The news producer at Action 12! back in Canyon Pointe laughed. "At least, let me ask before you blast me."

"I told you from the beginning of my contract with the station I cannot comment on my legal clients," Aisha snapped.

"I'm not asking for anything." Nella's tone turned sober. "I'm checking on a friend who's in Atlanta for her brother's wedding."

"And that's part of the story." Aisha smirked at Harri.

"Another part is the Guidestar stock price is tanking after hitting an all-time high for an IPO," Nella said. "Essie's already got a source from the SEC stating they're looking at your future sister-in-law for insider trading."

Harri bit her lower lip to keep from saying every bad word she knew.

Aisha closed her eyes and exhaled. "Thanks for the notice. I definitely owe you a huge favor."

"I know," Nella said. "I'll talk to you when you get back to Canyon Pointe."

Aisha ended the call and stared at Harri. "Now, we know the reason for sabotaging the wedding."

"This is way worse than we thought." Harri poked the speed dial for Tim.

"Hey, Harri," her boyfriend said cheerily. "Decided to join us for some sightseeing?"

"No." She swallowed hard. "This is a law office emergency. I need you all to come back to the hotel now. Someone's setting Renata up to take the fall for insider trading and fraud, and they're using Mister Spectacular to do it."

CHAPTER 29

Aisha leaned back in the armchair she'd claimed and stared at her laptop propped on her legs resting on the ottoman. For once, she was glad Harri insisted on the extra expense of the suites. However, she was pissed circumstances dictated she work on her first day off since her honeymoon last year.

She'd already sent out a press release that Mister Spectacular was merely talking to a friend who was about to get married and they were discussing which scriptures he'd read from the Bible during the ceremony. The excuse sucked, but it was the best she could do given the circumstances.

With Guidestar Healthcare, Inc., going public today, they had to list stock owners with the Securities and Exchange Commission. Renata had gotten a huge bonus at the end of the company's fiscal year. Some was in cash, but the majority was in stocks. Enough that her total holdings was on par with the three largest shareholders. She stood to make millions if the stock had held its price.

Unless she'd been involved in a short sell. Renata was too smart to do something that stupid. Nor would she ruin her reputation and put her relationship with Martin at risk. Aisha wanted to kick herself to even think of such a thing, but she had to look at all the factors so she wasn't blindsided again.

Susan had taken Lane with her to talk to the hotel manager. Hopefully, they could find out who was in the room across the hall from Renata's last Monday night. Susan seemed sure the manager would talk since both Lane and Renata's privacy had been violated. Not to mentioned the bad publicity the law firm could inflict on that particular hotel and the chain in general.

Harri and Rey watched the financial news outlets, looking for any indication of who might be behind the deliberate tanking of the stock price. Meanwhile, Tim and Arthur were furiously trying to trace the calls to the various wedding vendors.

LaShun, Jeremy, and Leo went to pick up Martin and hopefully get to Renata before anyone showed up to arrest her. That left Eric and Patty to keep the kids occupied though Devon and Jada weren't a bit fooled. They both loved Martin, Renata, and Lane, and they wanted to help. Unfortunately, there was little the older kids could do at this point.

Tim cursed and slammed his hand against the laminate top of the hotel room's desk. "Every one I've traced is a burner phone!"

"I've got one firm contact, but you're not going to like it," Arthur said.

"Any lead we can get would help," Aisha said.

"It's Renata office extension," he said mournfully.

"What's the time?" Tim leaned over the desk.

Arthur turned his laptop so Tim could see it. "One-nineteen on Friday."

"That corresponds with the call to the hotel's event manager about the reception," Harri said.

Aisha dropped her feet to the floor and set her laptop on the end table. She crossed over to the desk. "Most companies have security cameras outside the CEO's office."

Tim grinned at her hint. "It's a good thing Susan isn't here."

"Aisha could stick her fingers in her ears and sing 'La-la-la' if it would help," Arthur said.

Everyone looked at him. The poor man turned beet red. "I guess that wasn't a good joke."

Raucous laughter ensued, and Aisha patted Arthur's back.

"We're just shocked that you made a joke." She swiped at the tears of mirth. "But I would stick my fingers in my ears and sing if it would help you."

He shot her a shy smile. "Not really." He shifted the laptop back to face him. His fingers moved over the keys of his laptop with the grace and precision of a jazz master. After nearly fifteen minutes, he looked up from his screen. "I think we have something."

Arthur adjusted his laptop so Aisha and Tim could see the screen. Both Rey and Harri got up from the couch and stood beside Aisha to watch.

The screen showed Renata's assistant at her desk. She was white and looked to be in her late twenties to early thirties. Her dark hair was cut in a pixie style that complemented her oval face and thin build.

Time ticked away in the bottom right corner of the security recording. At one-fifteen, Renata strode out of her office. She handed a file to her assistant and spoke with the younger woman before she walked out of the shot. Three minutes later, Renata's assistant rose, walked into her boss's office, and closed the door.

The assistant walked out of the office five minutes later with Renata's white wedding planner. Aisha glanced at the kitchenette. The very same planner that currently sat on the counter.

After another seven minutes, the assistant walked into Renata's office with the book before she returned to her desk without it. She sat in her chair and calmly continued working. She smiled pleasantly at Renata when she returned with a bag from a local sub shop roughly ten minutes later. The two women talked for a moment before Renata disappeared into her office.

Arthur stopped the playback and looked up at Aisha and Harri.

Aisha turned to her partner. "Are you going to throw a temper tantrum if my alter ego has a little talk with Renata's assistant?"

"You brought your superhero togs to your brother's wedding?" Harri stared at her with an expression of dismay.

"A variation." Aisha shrugged. "In case of an emergency. I think saving Martin's love life, Lane's reputation, and Renata's career all qualify as emergencies.

Harri pursed her lips for a moment before she said, "If I did object to this stunt, would it stop you?"

"Probably not," Aisha admitted.

Harri shook her head. "Just do me a favor, and take backup."

"Contact Glass," Rey said. "If you take Lane, there will be too many questions."

"Do you want me to call the Atlanta FBI office?" Harri asked.

Aisha frowned as she considered what information they had. "Not yet. So far, all we've got is a civil claim against her for messing with the wedding vendors, and even that's questionable since we've already done damage control." She shook her head. "We need to find out what's her connection to the shareholder who engineered this fiasco before we bring in the authorities."

Arthur scribbled on the pad of paper beside him and tore off the sheet. "Here's her personal information."

Aisha glanced at the information. "How long has she been working for Renata?"

"Since January when Renata's long-time assistant retired," Arthur answered. "I'll see about any connections between her and the other major shareholders."

Rey wrapped his arm around her and pulled her close. "Be careful. You don't have your Kevlar with you."

"I think I can handle one back-stabby assistant," she muttered.

"But the back-stabby assistant probably isn't working alone." Rey tilted her chin up to face him. "I know you want to save your baby brother, but don't underestimate this woman."

Tim spoke up. "Maybe you should wait to discuss this with Renata before you go off half-cocked."

Harri tilted her head and stared at her boyfriend. "When the hell did you become Mister Cautious?"

Tim held up his hands. "I agree someone's out to destroy Renata's reputation and career." He pointed at Arthur's laptop. "But she may have asked her assistant to make copies of something in the notebook. I hate to point this out, but modern copy machines keep digital versions of what they copy in their memory."

"For how long?" Aisha asked.

Tim shrugged. "Depends on the model, the programming, and the amount of memory in its computer."

"All I'm going to do is talk to her for now." Aisha sighed. "It would be better if Mother Defiant was here. And I really never thought I'd say that in my lifetime."

CHAPTER 30

Harri had drafted Rey for a dinner run to a French-style café down the street from the hotel. When they got back to the hotel, LaShun and her crew had returned from retrieving Renata from Guidestar's corporate headquarters.

Poor Renata sat on one of the couches in Harri and Tim's suite, a stunned expression on her face. Martin sat next to her, holding her hand and fuming.

Harri carried her bags to the coffee table before she joined LaShun and Jeremy in the kitchenette where they were mixing margaritas. "How bad was it?"

"Between me pretending to be a lawyer and threatening to sue everyone for not letting me talk to my client face-to-face, and the guys going full queen mode and screaming at security, we finally got to Renata's office." LaShun squeezed a lime with a manual juicer until it was nothing more than damp pulp. "Bless her heart, Renata was trying to do damage control on the IPO, but it wasn't until the CFO told her about the ENN story that she realized just how bad things were. Also, Tim filled us in on what y'all discovered."

Harri stared at the bartending paraphernalia. "Where did you get all this stuff?"

"Janson was more than glad to donate a few things to the Estevez-Franklin cause," Jeremy said airily.

"Who the hell is Janson?" Harri said.

"Mr. Bernecki? The hotel's special event manager?" Jeremy said before he slapped the lid on the blender and turned on the device. When the margaritas were thoroughly mixed, he shut off the blender and added, "When he heard he wasn't the only one jacked around by our pain-in-the-ass wedding saboteur, he also gave me the tequila at wholesale."

As much as she wanted a shot of the liquor, Harri inhaled deeply and let out her breath. "Don't pour any for me."

"You sure?" Jeremy raised an eyebrow.

"No, one attorney needs to stay sober in case we need to post bail for the Owl and Glass." Harri leaned against the counter. Aisha's idea of confronting Renata's assistant didn't help the crawling sensation under her skin.

"Don't worry, Jaye." LaShun patted him on the back. "I'll drink hers."

Jeremy poured, and LaShun popped straws into the first two glasses and carried them over to Renata and Martin. Harri followed and perched on the ottoman.

"You two feel up to talking," she asked.

"Aisha should have waited for me," Martin snarled.

"Why? So you could get arrested for assault and battery?" Harri snapped.

"I don't need my big sisters to fight my fights," he growled.

Renata turned to him. "And I don't need you to fight my fights either." Her voice carried the same frigid tone Tim's did when he was positively furious.

"This is one case where it's best if you both let the law firm do your fighting for you," Harri said. They both opened their mouths to protest, but Harri held up her hands. "We have a question about your assistant."

"You mean Emily?" Renata cocked her head.

Harri nodded. "Did you ever tell her to do anything with your wedding planner? Like make copies of anything or make phone calls for you?"

Renata shook her head vigorously. "No. Most definitely not. I didn't want to be one of those executives who abused their staff by telling them to do personal errands."

"Arthur, you want to show her the clip?" Harri said.

Their IT manager had hooked his laptop up to the big screen TV in the room so everyone could see. The same security footage from before played. When the video got to the part where Emily walked out of Renata's office with her wedding planner, an inarticulate sound of rage exploded from Renata.

"Does she know Spanish?" LaShun asked.

"No." Renata made a face. "I offered to have the company pay for classes if she wanted to learn. Part of the expansion—" Her jaw snapped shut.

"Ms. Estevez, you are surrounded by your family and the best attorneys I know," Arthur said. "Anything you know could be relevant to what is happening, and none of it will leave this room."

Renata considered his words for a moment before she said, "The plan for the IPO cash influx is expansion into the Mexican markets."

"That puts a new wrinkle in our list of suspects," Harri muttered.

"I don't understand what Emily messing with our wedding has to do with today's IPO," Martin grumbled.

"Someone was trying to set Renata up to take the fall for the drop in the stock price," Harri explained patiently. "Someone who made a shit-ton of money today by shorting their Guidestar stock. Screwing with your wedding vendors was going to be their excuse to blame everything on your fiancée. Aisha having Lane check on you was just the cherry on the sundae."

"But how would they know where I was, much less Lane was coming to check on me?" Renata protested.

"Like Harri just said, Lane was a fortuitous accident for them," Tim growled as he strode over to the couches with Renata's phone and handed it to her. "As for how they found you, they bugged your phone."

Harri swore under her breath. "Please tell me it wasn't Corvus."

"No, this code was from Nightwatch," Tim said. "They call themselves a private security company, but they're really mercenaries. Anyone can buy their services if they have the money." He looked at Renata. "Someone really doesn't like you because these guys do not come cheap."

"But you removed the spyware, right?" Harri asked.

"Not before I cloned her phone." Tim grinned. "I figure we can have a little fun with these guys and keep them out of the way until the wedding's over."

"Oh, no." A horrified expression took over Renata's face. "I can't leave for our honeymoon on Sunday. I've got to deal with this mess at work."

"We'll do whatever you need us to do, babe." Martin drew her hand to his lips and kissed the back. "And I'll give you whatever you need."

Renata smiled at him and drew a deep breath before she faced Harri. "It would have to be one of the board members or possibly Dexter Fallon, the previous CEO. They're the only ones I know with that kind of money besides my parents."

"What if it's not someone at Guidestar?" LaShun said as she delivered more margaritas to the rest of the crew. "What if a rival company is the one who hired Nightwatch?"

"That could be anyone across the country," Arthur blurted. He held his hand up when LaShun offered him a margarita, so she sipped it instead before she sat down on the couch on Renata's free side.

"No." Harri shook her head. "Trying to ruin the wedding is too personal. And the succession of events is too damn convenient. It's got to be someone here in Atlanta."

"Everything depends on what the Ghost Owl and Glass can get out of Renata's assistant," Tim murmured.

Deep down, Harri knew he was right, but it gnawed on her that she couldn't do more. Because if Aisha couldn't get Renata's assistant Emily to talk, their brother's fiancée was in deep doggie doo.

CHAPTER 31

Aisha was forced to improvise when it came to her Ghost Owl gear. She could bring her reversible leather jacket and boots with her on the plane, but she didn't dare risk the tech Arthur and Tim developed in her helmet and gloves, much less her full suit, in the not-so-gentle care of the TSA or the airport baggage handlers. Luckily, the entire team could put their comms in their carry-on bags because they resembled many manufacturer's wireless earbuds.

She stopped at a costume supply shop and bought a replica of her Ghost Owl helmet, gloves, and pants. If she told any of her clients licensing their costume designs for adults would come in handy for them, they all would have laughed their butts off. Right now, she was damn glad she had.

Aisha arrived at Glass's building, grabbed the bags containing her makeshift costume, and took the private elevator to the penthouse. For once, she was thankful for LaShun and Jeremy's obsessions with wigs and hats. If anyone viewed the footage from the security camera in the atrium, they wouldn't be able to see her face.

When she reached the penthouse, Glass was already suited up and waiting for her. The other super's translucent hair on the right side blended with her white mask and unitard. She still shaved the left side of her head despite Aisha's recommendation for a less striking cut. Glass claimed the plunging neckline and her ample breasts distracted everyone from her hair.

"Let me get this straight because Harri was talking a mile a minute on the phone." Glass cocked her head. "You want me to be invisible while you question a secretary about insider trading in her company because she took her boss's wedding planner?"

"That was the end result of this mess," Aisha tossed her bags on Glass's lavender-colored couch. "Someone is setting up my brother's fiancée Renata to take the fall for illegal stock manipulation."

"Wait a minute!" Glass's eyes widened behind her mask. "Renata Estevez, the CEO the paparazzi caught with Lane? And your brother is Martin Franklin, the music producer?"

"You know them?" Aisha asked as she pulled her t-shirt over her head.

"Well, I only heard of Estevez when the news about her and Lane broke at mid-morning on ENN," Glass said. "But I've been following Franklin's career for the last five years. He has a knack for picking acts that are so awesome and danceable."

"Most people don't pay attention to the producers." Aisha kick off her canvas shoes and yanked down her shorts.

Glass shrugged. "But if you study music in the U.S. over the last century, you start to see patterns in certain areas based on the producers."

"Did you want to be a singer?" Aisha reached for her fake uniform pants.

"I think every kid dreams of getting attention for being special." Glass hugged herself. "In my case, I literally broke my vocal cords when my powers manifested the first time during choir practice in junior high." Her chuckle was rather self-deprecating. "The surgeon did the best he could to repair the damage when I returned to flesh and blood, but now, I sound like a phone sex operator." She sighed. "When I'm in my glass form and music is playing, it is truly better than sex."

"So, what you're really saying is my brother is a pimp, you're a john, and his clients are the hoes." Aisha fastened the new pants.

Glass laughed. The super was right. She could give Lauren Bacall or Kathleen Turner a run for their money in the throaty voice department.

"So what does the assistant stealing the wedding planner have to do with illegal stock trading?" Glass asked.

"Someone was trying to distract Renata from the IPO sabotage by attempting to cancel all her reservations." Aisha sat on the couch to pull on her socks and boots. "They didn't count on the bridesmaids taking over all the arrangements while the bride dealt with this IPO, which was arbitrarily moved up to the week of her wedding."

"They also didn't count on a super attorney being one of the brides-maids either." Glass perched on the edge of the matching lavender Queen Anne's chair.

"Or that two of the bridesmaids are the attorneys for the gentleman they used to trash my soon-to-be sister-in-law's reputation," Aisha fin-ished.

"I saw the pictures," Glass said sympathetically. "Is everything okay between Ms. Estevez and your brother?"

"Yeah, they're united in their anger." Aisha stood and slung on her jacket. "I'm more worried about Lane."

"So the rumor is true?" A delighted expression filled Glass's face. "He met someone?"

"I can neither confirm nor deny any such thing." Aisha picked up her fake helmet and gloves.

"It's still awesome." Glass clapped her hands. "I'm so happy he found someone."

"You can tease him about it later," Aisha said. "Right now, I've got an executive assistant to speak with before Renata gets arrested by the local FBI office."

Emily's address was in an apartment complex in the suburb of Alpharetta. Aisha carried Glass as she flew, and in turn, Glass formed a force field bubble around them so no photographers could get a clear picture of them.

From the satellite maps Arthur had pulled up, the balcony for Emily's apartment faced a wooded area. It made sense to approach from that angle to avoid other residents.

Luckily, the curtains over the sliding glass doors were closed when Aisha landed on the balcony. She set Glass on her feet. The other superhero immediately faded from view.

Aisha knocked on the door. Rustling sounds came from further inside the apartment, followed by a woman's and then a man's voices. She knocked again.

The curtain shifted, and the dark-haired young woman from the security video of Renata's office peered around the edge of the fabric. The real-life version had disheveled hair, and she wore a pink terrycloth robe. Her eyes widened at the sight of Aisha in her fake superhero togs.

"You can open the door, or I can accidentally break it while knocking." Aisha smiled sweetly behind her visor. Thankfully, Tim rigged a voice modulator for her, so she still sounded like the Ghost Owl with the fake mask. Even though Renata's assistant couldn't see her expression, it helped with the tone Aisha wanted to convey.

Emily eased the sliding door open a sliver. She clutched her bathrobe at the neck and waist, a sure sign she'd been in the middle of entertaining someone in her bedroom. "Who are you?"

"Really? You don't recognize me?" Aisha shook her head. "I definitely need to talk to my agent."

Emily stiffened, and dark pink suffused her cheeks. "If you're really the Ghost Owl, what are you doing here in Atlanta?"

"Ironically, I'm in town for your boss's wedding. And I need to talk to you about why you took her wedding planner and returned it."

"I-I didn't take anything of Ms. Estevez's!"

"Ah, so you forgot about the security camera aimed at her door, and subsequently your desk?"

Emily slumped against the edge of the sliding door. "Did she send you here to fire me?"

"No, I just want to talk to you for a few minutes because I think you were used by—"

Movement flashed behind Emily. Something metallic gleamed in the setting sun.

"Glass!" Aisha shoved the door fully open and grabbed Emily, twisting to shield the assistant's body with her own.

Bullets ripped through the curtains and bounced off the other superhero's force field. One shot missed them entirely and shattered the glass in the sliding doors. The abrupt silence was followed by the clicking sound of an empty chamber.

"Watch her," Aisha ordered. She plunged past the drapes.

In a desperate move, the shooter threw his gun at her before he bolted toward the apartment's front door. She grabbed the shooter and hauled him into the middle of the living room.

"Let me go! Let me go!" When that didn't get Aisha to release him, he screamed, "My dad will sue you! You'll never be a superhero again!"

"Glass," she called out. "I've got him. You two okay out there?"

"We're fine." Glass created a little force field on the concrete and carpet so Emily could walk inside without slicing up her feet.

Renata's assistant glared at the man in Aisha's grip. "What the hell, Kyle? You tried to kill me!"

"Kyle?" Aisha looked at the man who seemed about the same age as Emily. "Kyle Haynes?"

He wisely clamped his jaw shut while Emily struggled against Glass's grip in her desire to attack her lover.

Aisha groaned. "The FBI are going to love this."

Chapter 32

Harri couldn't help laughing hysterically while Aisha relayed the events at Emily's apartment. The rest of the law office staff remained quiet though Susan wore a smirk that indicated Aisha was in for a night of teasing when she returned.

"How long are you going to be there?" Harri asked.

"I still need to give a statement to the Alpharetta Police Department." Her sigh whistled over the phone receiver. "Probably another hour or two. You guys go ahead and eat without me. I'll stop and pick up something on my way back."

Harri didn't have the heart to say she'd already made the meal run.

"Be careful," Rey called out.

"I will." Aisha ended the call.

Lane turned to his girlfriend, sitting beside him on the couch. "See, Jess? This had absolutely nothing to do with me other than trying to be a good friend."

Jessica shot a weird look at Renata on the other couch before she turned to Harri. "Y'all couldn't have asked someone else to check on her?"

"Lane was the only non-family member we trusted not to make the situation worse than it was," Harri said.

Renata turned to Martin. "And I really am sorry I left you a note and took off like that. I should have handled things better."

"Baby, you've been trying too hard to make this wedding perfect." Martin pulled her in the crook of his right arm. "I should have seen what both the wedding planning and the business planning were doing to you. I'm sorry I didn't, and I promise to do better."

"We've got everything you need to present to the board of directors tonight," Tim announced as he stood from his chair at the suite's desk. "Everything's backed up in triplicate, so there's no way Nightwatch can bury their involvement in this fiasco." He crossed the room and handed Renata the flash drive.

"Especially when the FBI can subpoena the hotel's records if the manager tries to back out of testifying that Nighthawk personnel were in the room across from yours," Susan added.

Renata turned to Lane. "I am so sorry you got caught in my mess. You were trying to make sure I was all right, and I do appreciate it."

"No problem." He looked at Jessica. "Now can I dance with the bride at the wedding?"

"I'll think about it." But a ghost of a smile played along the woman's mouth.

"We need to get going if we're going to make it to Atlanta One News for their special live report." Lane stood and held out his hand to Jessica. "You sure you're ready to go public, honey?"

She took his hand and let him pull her to her feet. "Yes. Definitely. I don't want any more misunderstandings between us or anyone else."

"See y'all at the wedding." Lane said cheerily. He and Jessica both waved before they left the suite.

A minute later, there was a knock on the door. Harri crossed the room to open it. Rey and Jeremy entered, but Harri couldn't help staring at the ill-fitting costume Rey wore. It was tight. Too tight. It would be a toss-up on whether Aisha would stroke out first at seeing it or Rey's costume pants would split open on the backside.

"Oh, my god!" Harri gestured wildly. "Jeremy! I can't let a client go out in public looking like this!"

"It's the best I could do on short notice, Harriet Mathilda!" Jeremy yelled back. "Your licensee doesn't make Black Falcon costumes in the sizes the real Black Falcon wears!"

Rey pulled off the helmet. "Thanks, Harri." He waved indignantly at Jeremy. "I told him I have a pair of black jeans in my suitcase. I don't want to do a Skyball and lose what little dignity in the supers game I've regained."

Harri scrubbed her hands down her face. "Please put on the jeans. Do you have your favorite hoodie with you, too?"

"Yep." The kid grinned at her.

She made a shooing motion with her hand. "For the love of god, please go put those on."

He darted out of the hotel suite before anyone else could make a comment.

Tim crossed his arms. "Jeremy, what were you thinking? No super wants to do a Skyball. Not even Ultramegaperson."

"Hey! I did the best I could with the materials at hand!" Jeremy gesticulated wildly. "I'm not at my workshop, and it's not like any super can waltz past the TSA as a regular citizen with their gear. Next time, have Aisha and Rey fly here on their own power, instead of screaming at me!"

A piercing whistle rent the air. Everyone stared at Renata.

"That's enough! From all of you!" She jumped to her feet and slashed the air with her right hand. "Y'all have been bickering since you got here, and I've got more than enough shit on my plate between the mothers, my board of directors, and then my own assistant trying to ruin my wedding!"

She stomped over and faced Jeremy. "I know you did what you

could, but even you had to realize the only person who' be happy about those damn pants on Rey would be Aunt Queenie."

Renata turned on Harri. "I know you are worse about bossing everyone around than either Betty or LaShun—"

"Hey!" LaShun protested.

"Shut up. I'll get to you in a minute," Renata snapped before she turned back to Harri. "Guess what? I'm not excited about Aisha and Rey moving to Paris for a whole year either. I was looking forward to Martin and me visiting Canyon Pointe a little more often once this stupid IPO was out of the way.

"But this studying abroad is important to Rey's career. If I can suck it up for a year, you can, too. And if this is about money, hell, I'll buy you a damn plane ticket so you can visit."

"I have the money," Harri grumbled. She really wanted to yell back at Renata, but the woman had a point. Maybe, Harri was the one being a selfish bitch in this scenario.

"You!" Renata whirled around and jabbed a finger in Tim's direction. "I don't know what your problem is, but I've got a pretty good idea. So either do it or don't do it, but quit moping about it!"

Tim's face turned as dark red as his hair. Obviously, there was something going on Harri didn't know about. For an instant, she feared he was planning on moving out of the loft.

He walked over to her and wrapped his arms around her. "I'm not going anywhere," he whispered against her hair.

"But—"

"I'll tell you later," he murmured. "Now's not the time."

"LaShun—" Renata's face abruptly softened. "Thanks for being the best matron of honor I could ever want." The two women hugged, and tears started to flow.

"Arthur and Susan—" Renata sniffed, and she still had a tight grip on LaShun when she looked at the pair. "Thank you for helping me clear my name without giving me any extra headaches in the process."

"If you're finished carrot and sticking all of us, go fix your make-up," Harri said. "We've got a corporation to set right."

Harri couldn't remember the last time she was in a limo. Renata called the corporation's car service because Tim's didn't trust Nighthawk not to mess with Renata's personal vehicle or their rental minivan. She and Tim sat silently in the back with Martin and Renata while Rey did aerial reconnaissance overhead. Their driver had been tickled to work with a super.

Her nerves could have been dipped in acid the way everything in her body twitched. She didn't like this plan, but Renata made the call because it was her career on the line. But after Kyle Haynes took pot shots at Aisha and Glass, not to mention his girlfriend, Harri didn't trust his father not to pull a similar stunt in the Guidestar corporate conference room.

"You need to calm down," Tim whispered.

"Did your dad ever drag you into corporate board meetings?" she asked.

"All the time," he said in a disgusted tone.

"Grandma did the same with me." Harri stared out the window before she looked at him again. "I think she knew Dad would never be able to handle the business. I think Dad knew too, which is why he sold it."

"Your grandmother ruled Winters, Inc., with an iron fist, so why the jitters?" he asked.

"Because when she was in charge, she made me read the dossiers of everyone involved, and I had to figure out what each person would do." Harri's chuckle was self-deprecating. "When I was in grade school, I thought it was a game, but when I understood the real-world ramifications . . ."

"She wasn't evil, Harri," Tim said. "She was trying to teach you how the real world works."

"Maybe that's the problem." Harri looked into his dark blue eyes. "The world shouldn't be that cynical."

Harri resorted to Patty's stupid meditation breathing exercises to calm herself down before they arrived at Guidestar's corporate headquarters. They exited the limo, and Renata gave their driver strict orders to remain in front of the building.

She repeated that order to the security guard manning the desk at the entrance. He nodded and gave her an affirmative. He also warned her the board of directors had arrived early and were upstairs, waiting for her.

They followed Renata onto the express elevator to the top floors. She and Martin were no longer touching, much less acting all lovey-dovey. They both had their game faces on.

In Martin's case, it was just weird. Harri had never seen this side of him before. He'd always been the bratty younger brother who followed her, Aisha, and Jeremy around the Franklins' old neighborhood in Canyon Pointe. But he didn't have Marvin's quiet surety either. Martin was more . . . intense.

The elevator doors slid open, and Renata marched with determination straight into the conference room. More than the board of directors sat or stood in the spacious room. Including a man and a woman wearing FBI lanyards. Harri didn't acknowledge Special Agent Cutler, nor did Cutler make any indication she knew Harri. They had spoken earlier today, and Harri had already sent the FBI agent copies of the evidence they'd collected so far.

"This is a private corporate meeting, Ms. Estevez," one of the old men barked. "Get rid of that hooligan!"

"That hooligan is Black Falcon." Renata glanced up at Rey. "He rather insisted on accompanying me because he and my personal attorney Harri Winters discovered someone here hired a private military service called Nightwatch to spy on me."

Renata marched around the table and snapped her fingers at the man sitting in what obviously should have been her seat. "Move it," she barked.

He turned beet red and didn't even have the balls to argue. Instead, he jumped out the chair and edged past the male FBI agent with Cutler.

Renata glared at the man in the chair to the right of hers. He scrambled out of it without a word. She inclined her head to Harri, who didn't have to be told twice. The sweet lady who was marrying Harri's foster brother was as commanding in the board room as Grandma Harri.

Tim and Martin framed Black Falcon behind the CEO.

However, Renata remained standing at the head of the table. "Ladies and gentlemen, Guidestar has a fox in the henhouse. One who deliberately sabotaged today's IPO."

"We already know who sabotaged the IPO." The white-haired elderly gentleman sitting directly opposite of Renata sneered. "It was you." He waved at the FBI agents. "They're here to arrest you."

The smile Renata gave the man would have terrified a great white shark. "Did they tell you that, Fletcher?"

Uncertainty flashed across Fletcher Haynes' face, but it was quickly replaced by an arrogant expression. "I'm not the chairman of the board. Garfield, would you care to detail the charges we discussed?"

"Failure of the principal to fulfill their fiduciary duty to the corporation," Garfield Lansing, chairman of Guidestar Healthcare's board, read dryly from the sheet of paper in front of him. "Using the corporation's initial public offering for the principal's fraudulent personal gain. Manipulating the corporation's stock price, again for the principal's fraudulent personal gain. Not to mention the principal violating numerous SEC rules to the detriment of the corporation, et cetera, et cetera."

He looked over at the FBI agents. "Special Agent Cutler, it's my understanding from our previous conversation a third party has delivered evidence to you."

"Yes, sir," Cutler answered crisply.

"And have your people made any arrests in this matter?" Lansing continued.

"Two so far, sir, Emily Norton, Ms. Estevez's executive assistant has been very cooperative in return for reduced charges." Cutler's teeth shone in a feral grin. "And her accomplice Kyle Haynes added to your principal's crimes with conspiracy to commit murder with Kyle's attempts to kill Ms. Norton, Glass, and the Ghost Owl having been ordered by your principal."

Everyone at the table turned to look at Fletcher Haynes. His initial glee turned to fury. He jumped to his feet and yanked a gun from his pocket.

All amusement at the situation disappeared from Harri. She groaned. "This is getting ridiculous. We really need gun control in this country."

"Put the gun down, Haynes!" Cutler yelled. Both she and her partner had their weapons drawn and pointed at Fletcher.

Harri looked up at Tim. "I want a watch like the one you gave Susan."

Her boyfriend looked like he wasn't sure whether to laugh or yell at her.

"Shut up! All of you are idiots!" Fletcher yanked on the jacket collar of the female board member next to him, but instead of scared, she looked pissed as hell.

He pushed her forward toward the head of the table. Martin stepped back.

"Get out of the way, Falcon," Fletcher snarled.

"I can't let you leave, sir." Rey was all earnest boy scout. He lowered his voice though it was so quiet in the room everyone could hear everything. "The FBI gets rather upset with supers who let bad guys get away."

Fletcher brought his gun to bear on Rey, which was probably the kid's plan. "Damn, immigrants! You think you're going to take over—"

"Shut up, Fletcher!" The female board member stomped on Fletcher's foot and darted for Rey.

Before anyone else could react, Martin knocked the gun out of Fletcher's hand with his own left and threw a right punch straight at Fletcher Haynes' face. The board member's nose broke with an audible snap.

Fletcher muttered muffled obscenities while he tried to staunch the gush of blood. Rey pulled Martin out of the way while Cutler and her partner cuffed the disgraced board member.

"Black Falcon, Ms. Winters, we'll be in touch," Cutler said in a clipped cadence before they hauled Fletcher out of the conference room.

"Ms. Estevez, I think we can deal with the corporate clean-up in the morning." Mr. Lansing smiled. "I think we've all had more than enough excitement for today. Though for clarity's sake what exactly is your relationship with Mister Spectacular?"

"He's a friend of my family," Martin snapped. "What was left out of the pictures Fletcher Haynes' lackies circulated was that I was in the hotel room with my fiancée." He took two steps, grasped Renata's hand, and kissed it before he faced Mr. Lansing again. "We asked him to read some scripture at our wedding. However, the spa night I arranged for me and my lady was the one night Lane had free to go over what we wanted him to read.

"So, Haynes wasn't thinking when he targeted Renata Estevez. My friends are now her friends because we will share everything in our new life. The rest of you better remember that."

Harri's eyes burned at Martin's passionate statement. Could she take that kind of chance with Tim?

Chapter 33

"Initially, the Alpharetta PD wasn't real pleased with the FBI claiming jurisdiction, but the sergeant in charge realized Kyle might get off thanks to his family's influence if the case stayed local." Aisha shrugged before she smacked Rey's fingers as he tried to steal more of her ribs while she sat on the couch in her own suite. "The peach cobbler's in the fridge, baby. Leave me some protein."

"I'm eating my feelings because you and your brother beat up all the bad guys today, and I didn't get to," Rey complained. But he got up from the couch and trudged to the kitchenette. "Anyone want some?"

Both Harri and Tim declined. Harri looked around the room. "Where is my godson? He should be awake right now."

"Spending the night with his cousins over at Mom and Dad's," Aisha said as she ripped off another meaty bone from her last slab of ribs. "They offered to take Grace, too, but Arthur said two kids in diapers was too much for overnight. I think Mom's feeling a little guilty about her blow-up on Saturday."

She dug her fork into her potato salad. "What's the status of Renata's job? Some boards don't take to lightly stock drops that bad, even though none of it was her fault."

"She and the rest of the board have a lot of clean-up to do." Harri shrugged. "But they seem willing to keep her for now."

"Come on, Harri," Tim said. "Even I know they can't fire her without a huge discrimination lawsuit after Fletcher Haynes' diatribe about immigrants."

"Hey, if she wants to stay there, that's her business," Harri retorted. "Personally, I think she's looking at building up the stock and then jumping ship. There's a lot of companies that would love someone with her expertise at the helm."

"I know I would," Rey said around a mouthful of peach cobbler as he sat down next to Aisha with the whole aluminum-foil pan. She was rather glad she picked up a full cobbler rather than the individual servings from the barbeque joint.

Aisha laughed. "Baby, you can't afford Renata."

"Not yet, but eventually." He waggled his eyebrows, so she stole a bite of cobbler.

"By the way, I saw Lane and his girlfriend's interview on Atlanta One tonight." She pointed the full fork at Harri. "Nice prepping, girl! I knew you'd get the hang of the PR side."

"I learned from the best." Her head dropped against the back of the chair. "Think we can get through the rest of this week's events without needing any superheroics?"

Aisha laughed hysterically. "Really? With our luck?"

Rey reached over and snatched a rib before she could stop him.

"Hey! Stop it!" Aisha punched his bicep. He noisily chew the meat off the bone.

Harri stood and Tim followed suit. "After this day, I am sleeping in tomorrow."

"Not for too long," Aisha said as the other couple headed for the door.

Harri pivoted, her eyes narrowed. "If LaShun wakes me up before noon about those damn place cards for the reception, I will shove every single one of her wigs down her throat."

"And if it's Jeremy?" Aisha grinned.

"I will shove his wigs in the opposite direction," Harri growled.

"He'd like it too much." Aisha laughed.

"Good night." Tim steered Harri through the hotel room door. She was definitely tired if she couldn't come up with a rejoinder before he hustled her out of the hotel suite.

"You know, with Mitch at your parents tonight, I can think of a few interesting things to do with the peach cobbler." Rey flashed a lecherous smile.

"So can I." Aisha leaned in for her husband's kiss. She hoped her little brother was as happy as she was.

Chapter 34

Harri leaned against the bathroom door of their suite, her arms crossed, while Tim brushed his teeth.

He caught her reflection in the mirror and asked "Wod's wong?" around his mouthful of suds and the brush.

"Not a damn thing." She didn't remember ever feeling this deeply in love with Eddie. Part of her regretted how she had wasted ten years trying to be something she wasn't for him. It hadn't been fair to herself any more than it had been to Eddie.

Tim spit into the sink and rinsed his mouth. He turned to face her as he dried his face and hands.

"You've never looked at me like that before." He tossed the hand towel on the counter and leaned his forearm on the doorjamb above her head. "Usually, I can figure out what you're thinking."

"Maybe it's because I've never really felt this way before." She wrapped her arms around his bare skin above his pajama bottoms. "I love you, Tim Canyon." She sucked in a deep breath before she added, "I don't have a ring for you yet, but would you marry me?"

His face softened. "Yes, Harri Winters. I will."

He lowered his mouth to hers. His kiss was passionate and sweet and a host of other things she couldn't name.

When they parted, she said, "Do you mind if we don't tell anyone until we get home? After we bitched Betty out about wedding etiquette, I really don't want to do anything more to cast a shadow over Martin and Renata's nuptials."

Tim chuckled. "I'm glad we're on the same page." This time, his kiss turned into something else entirely.

And Harri was glad she had already put the "Do Not Disturb" sign on their hotel door.

CHAPTER 35

On Saturday evening, Aisha swayed with Martin on the dance floor at the hotel's ballroom. "Your lady puts on one hell of a wedding."

Her brother glanced at Renata, who danced with Rey a few feet away. "She's the best thing that's ever happened to me." Martin smiled at Aisha. "Would you mind a little company in Paris next year?"

"You are always welcome, but you're leaving for Europe tomorrow," Aisha said.

"Renata's going to have to stay here in Atlanta for a while." He grimaced. "Some of the minority shareholders are screaming bloody murder over the Haynes shorting the company stock even though they've both been arrested. But leave it to Renata to negotiate a bump in salary and a hell of a bonus if she can pull the company out of its current tailspin." He glanced at his bride again and grinned. "If anyone can, it's my lady."

Aisha laughed. "What are you going to do while she's saving a bunch of rich white folks?"

"I've got a new act in the studio right now. You would not believe the pipes on this girl," Martin said.

"Can I get a copy of her album before it's released?" Aisha wheedled.

He leaned away. "What's your game?"

"It's for Glass." At his confused expression, she added, "She's actually a big fan of yours, and she saved Emily's life."

"You mean the bitch who tried to destroy my wedding?"

"Without Emily, we couldn't have cleared Renata," Aisha pointed out. "And without Glass, I wouldn't have Emily."

"All right," he conceded. "But if she leaks it before the drop date, I will dox the bitch."

"Warning taken."

Jeremy approached them. "You've had your time, girl. My turn."

Martin laughed and released Aisha. He dramatically swept Jeremy in his arms and dipped him before the pair launched in a ballroom tango that didn't match the ballad the quartet was playing at all.

Rey wrapped his arm around her waist and pulled her to him. She caught a glimpse of Leo dancing with the bride before her own husband guided her into a waltz that fit the music.

"Is it me or has Harri been acting weird the last few days?" Rey whispered.

"Either they had some really good sex after your confrontation with Haynes or Tim finally proposed," she murmured.

Rey grinned down at her. "As chickenshit as Tim's been, my money's on Harri proposing to him."

Aisha watched her best friend dance with her boyfriend before she looked up at Rey again. "Honestly, I don't care who asked who. I'm just glad to see her happy for once in her life."

Chapter 36

Six days later, cold ran down Aisha's spine that had nothing to do with the chill of the Lechuza Building's basement. She stared at Arthur. "Are you sure?"

He gestured at the terminal he was using in the basement computer lab. "Voice recognition says ninety-eight percent probability the person speaking was Byron Trubble."

"And the other two percent?" Harri asked.

"That would account for Trubble being under some kind of duress," Tim said.

"Why the hell would he call me for help?" Aisha threw her hands in the air.

"Because you wouldn't snap his neck on sight," Rey murmured. At her glare, he shrugged. "Baby, you're not a killer." Rey turned to Arthur. "And the odds that it's a trap?"

This time, Arthur shrugged. "I'd say fifty-fifty given the ladies witnessed Miss Purrception haul him away trussed up like a Thanksgiving turkey."

"Have any more hit teams been sent out through the NSB messenger system?" Aisha asked.

"Not since the Ghost Owl and Black Falcon captured Valentine Delante at the Federal court house." Arthur's frown deepened. "But we still don't know to whom Miss Purrception was delivering Trubble."

"Or if our third party was using the system to deliver untraceable communication like Corvus was," Tim added.

"Maybe we should put off Paris for a year, baby," Rey murmured.

"No, you are not putting off school for an entire year," Harri growled. "Look, I know I've been a shit lately. But Trubble's messed with our lives enough. No more. You are going to Paris."

"Yes, ma'am." Rey grinned.

Harri shook her index finger under his nose. "Just remember, you're taking the last bit of family I have left, Rey Garcia, and I expect you to bring her back in one piece."

"I will bring her and Mitch home, Harri." Rey reached for Aisha's hand and squeezed. "But may I point out, she's not your only family anymore? You've got everyone living in this building whether you like it or not."

Harri looked at the solitaire diamond on her left hand, and then Tim, before her attention returned to Rey. "I know that now. That's why we're waiting until you guys get back from Europe. I'm going to need my matron of honor at the wedding chapel in Vegas."

"Could we can all the girly stuff until later?" Aisha snapped. "What are we going to do about Trubble?"

"Honey, there's not a damn thing we can do," Harri said. "If Trubble can, he'll contact you again."

"And if he doesn't?" Aisha retorted.

Harri stared her dead in the eyes. "It means he's dead, and we've got an even bigger threat on our hands."

When Steve rescues a law school classmate from certain death at a holiday party, he accidentally exposes himself as a super. How can he have a normal life with his girlfriend and her family when the girl he saved and the paparazzi are chasing him all over Canyon Pointe? Turn the page for an exciting preview of *A Very Hero New Year*!

A Very Hero New Year

The party sounds got louder as Steve Connors jogged at a normal human speed up the southeast stairwell of the Canyon Pointe University Law School building. When he pushed open the steel door to the rooftop patio, the music and laughter ratcheted up several decibels. The December post-finals party was in full swing.

The dry wind off the western desert kept the traffic fumes at street level. That left the odor of alcohol and intoxicated humans at the top of the seven-story edifice to mix with the sage and creosote-scented breeze.

Bethany Spears from his Con law class waved, and he strode over to the study group who'd become his friends. Carter Swift slapped him on the shoulder and shoved a cup of beer into Steve's hand. "It's about time Mr. A-plus showed up." Carter looked around him. "Now where's the hottie you claim you're dating?"

"She took her son to her parent's for dinner tonight, and you can keep the cup." Steve pressed the red plastic back into his friend's hand. Carter's breath was enough to get everyone on the roof plastered.

Steve was more than a little disappointed Qiang refused to come. She claimed she got all her partying out of her system when she was an undergrad. The truth was situations like this underscored their age difference, and it made Qiang damn uncomfortable. Part of him understood. The rest of him tried to convince her no one would know her age unless she announced it.

For some reason, she didn't take that as the compliment he meant it to be.

Maybe, his perspective was skewed. People had always assumed he was older because of his size.

"I don't think this woman exists," Bethany remarked. "Unless Qiang is the nickname for your right hand."

"Oh, come on," Nick Lyons drawled. "For all you know, he could have bought one of those lifelike Japanese sex dolls."

Carter and Bethany roared with laughter.

Maybe it was a good thing Qiang didn't come after all. She would have electrocuted Nick's balls for saying that.

"Ha, ha." Steve rolled his eyes. "Thank you for proving her point she didn't want to spend a boring evening with a bunch of immature trust-fund babies."

"Hey, I resemble that remark." Carter waved his cup, sloshing beer over the side. "Maybe your mystery woman is really waiting for a rich and charming guy to sweep her off her feet."

"More like Prince Charming to sweep her floor," Nick shot back.

Steve snorted, and Bethany laughed out loud.

"I think I'll find something to drink before Carter washes the floor with all the beer." Steve headed for the corner where tables were set up with food, alcohol, and soft drinks.

He selected a plastic bottle of cola. The last thing he needed was to get drunk and accidentally display his powers. Though honestly, it would take every bit of beer and wine on the table to produce a slight buzz thanks to his metabolism.

For the last twelve years of his life, he'd been so careful to keep his secret, only to discover he had a twin with the exact same powers. A twin brother who was a noted and popular superhero.

A brother who despised him.

Steve stepped away from the crowd. The old guilt resurfaced though everyone told him Professor Paranoia kidnapping and controlling him wasn't his fault. Even Tim Canyon, AKA the original Ghost Owl, didn't blame Steve for the severe injuries he inflicted on the non-super. Tim was damn lucky he could walk again after what Steve had done. In fact, Tim insisted on training Steve in some basic self-defense techniques. Sparring with his brother Rey though often left him bruised despite his abilities.

Tim's lessons remained at the forefront of Steve's mind despite the festive atmosphere. He scanned the area. Red, green, and white lights lit up several buildings in downtown. A few other offices twinkled blue and white. Above all of them, the Del Oro Bank's red and gold eagle ruled the skyline.

A girl wearing a hoodie and jeans leaned against the retaining wall on the other side of the law school's roof. She wasn't staring at the lights of downtown. No, her head stretched over the edge of the ledge. A few of her braids waved in the breeze. There wouldn't be anything on that side of the building but the street, traffic, and pedestrians. The school didn't even have a door to enter on that side, so she couldn't be watching for someone who said they'd be here tonight.

Steve went back to the refreshment tables and grabbed a second bottle of cola. Before he strode halfway across the roof, the girl straightened and flung her right leg over the safety wall.

He raced toward her as fast as he could without using superspeed. "Hey—" Thankfully, she turned to look at him. Mariah Pendleton. She had been in several of his first year classes. Quiet, but she had the right answer every time one of the professors called on her.

"It's Mariah, right?" Steve said.

"Yeah." She looked at him suspiciously while she straddled the wall. A couple of her braids stuck out from beneath the hood of her sweatshirt. "Why aren't you with your friends, Connors?" A strong whiff of alcohol came from her.

"I went to get a drink, and I saw you over here by yourself." He held out one of the bottles of cola. "So I brought you one."

She shook her head. "Don't want it."

"I can get you orange? Root beer? Lemon-lime?"

"I don't want anything from you. Go away." Mariah looked down again and swung her other leg over the wall.

"Hey, that's kind of dangerous." Blood roared in his ears. Logic and debate he could handle. A drunk, distraught person planning to harm herself was way out of his wheelhouse.

"That's me. Stupid Mariah." A sob caught in her throat.

Steve looked back at the party. No one noticed what was going on over here, and he needed help. If he left to grab Bethany, Mariah would fall.

Or worse, jump.

He looked at Mariah who was studiously ignoring him in favor of the pavement. "You're not stupid, Mariah. You always know the answers when you're called on."

"Then why am I at the bottom of the class?" she wailed.

"We can all get the same exact score, and the profs still rank us," he said. "It's part of the stupidity of law school. We have to figure out what really matters."

"All that matters to my family is that I be the best." Mariah cried in earnest now. "I'm not. I can't go home."

Her pain infiltrated the scars of his heart. He understood. It didn't matter how much his adoptive parents loved him. He'd wondered his entire life why he wasn't good enough for his biological parents.

"Have you told them about your rank?" he asked.

"No." She hiccupped.

"Why does your rank matter more to your parents than whether you're learning the material?"

"Because they need to see the measurement." She gulped. "Because they told me if I wasn't in the top five percent, there was no reason to pay for my tuition."

"Wow," he muttered. "What a pair of douches."

"B-but they're right. I-I don't deserve the education if I can't do it."

"If money's an issue, I know a scholarship you could apply for." Steve edged over to the retaining wall and leaned against it. He peeked over the side. Yep, all concrete below. With her shaking and the amount of alcohol she had probably consumed, he needed to get her back on this side of the wall. "Why don't you come with me, and I can get the info for you?" He held out his free hand.

"Don't touch me!" she screeched.

"I won't if you climb back on this side of the wall," he assured her.

"Why would you care?" She finally looked at him. "Mister Top-of-the-Class," she spat.

"Maybe that's the difference," he said. "My parents don't really care about class rank. I don't have the same pressure on me that you do."

"Except you already have an internship with a firm," she said morosely.

Was that the real issue? She was jealous of him?

"Where did you hear that?" he asked.

"People talk." Mariah stared at the traffic below again.

"You do realize I'm working for my sister-in-law to pay for my room and board while I'm going to school, right?" he said dryly.

Mariah looked at him and sniffed. "You do realize that's still experience, right?"

Steve chuckled. "More like my brother got lucky, and his wife takes pity on me. Not to mention, it's a very small firm. They could use some help. I could set up a meeting—"

"I don't need your pity," Mariah snapped.

"It's not pity," he said. "Like I said rank is bullshit. You're the smartest person in our class. And my boss Harri would be the first one to say, 'What do you call someone who scores 675 on the Mojave bar exam?'"

"What?"

"A lawyer," he answered.

A slight giggle escaped from Mariah.

"And if you don't believe me, believe Harri. The bar exam has nothing to do with your class rank," he added. "And how you perform in the real world doesn't have anything to do with either of those things."

"I still don't want to go home for break." Mariah stared at the traffic below once again. "I can't face them, and I don't have any place to go."

"What if I find you a place to stay over break?" Steve said gently. "Would you climb back over the wall?"

Mariah sniffed again. "Like where?"

"I was going to offer the spare bedroom at my apartment," he said. "But if that is too weird for you, there are some other ladies in the building who would let you stay with them for a few days until we can figure something out."

"Okay." Mariah wiped at her eyes with the sleeve of her hoodie.

Some idiot blasted an air horn behind him. Mariah jerked. Her one hand on the retaining wall slipped from the concrete. In slow motion horror, he watched her drop.

Steve tossed aside the cola bottles, leapt over the retaining wall, and dived for the screaming Mariah.

Acknowledgements

First of all, I want to thank Elaina Lee for her fantastic cover and Jaye Manus for her interior design. These ladies make me look so professional and polished.

Thanks also go to Kate, Matt, Mel, and Tracie for our virtual writing time and their encouragement. It goes to show how much things have changed since COVID-19 hit the U.S. shores. I spend more time with people on the other side of the country than people in my own neighborhood.

Last, but not least, thank you to my husband, my son and his brand new family, and my co-writer and constant companion Bella. I love you all!

SUZAN HARDEN transitioned from writing information technology manuals for companies and legal articles for a law enforcement magazine to her first love, fantasy and science fiction in all their forms. She's the author of the Bloodlines, the 888-555-HERO, and the Justice series.